SLAM DUNK!

OTHER BOOKS BY SHARON ROBINSON

Fiction

Safe At Home

Nonfiction

Jackie's Nine: Jackie Robinson's Values to Live By

*Promises to Keep: How Jackie Robinson
Changed America*

Stealing Home

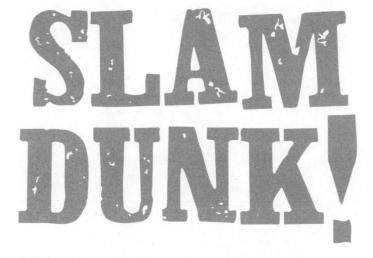

Sharon Robinson

SCHOLASTIC PRESS ■ NEW YORK

• Library of Congress Cataloging-in-Publication Data • Robinson, Sharon, 1950– Slam dunk! / by Sharon Robinson ; edited by Sheila Keenan. — 1st ed. p. cm. • Summary: At Harlem's Langston Hughes Middle School, eleven-year-old Elijah "Jumper" Breeze and his friends compete against Nia and her girlfriends on the basketball court, in a video dance tournament, and for a Student Council seat, and, meanwhile, several of the students face issues with their fathers. • ISBN-13: 978-0-439-67199-6 (hardcover: alk. paper) ISBN-10: 0-439-67199-X (hardcover: alk. paper) [1. Contests—Fiction. 2. Basketball—Fiction. 3. Family life—New York (N.Y.)—Fiction. 4. Friendship—Fiction. 5. Fathers—Fiction. 6. African Americans—Fiction. 7. New York (N.Y.)—Fiction.] I. Title. PZ7.R567583Sla 2007 [Fic]—dc22 2006102462 • 12 11 10 9 8 7 6 5 4 3 2 • 08 09 • Printed in the United States of America 23 • First edition, September 2007 • The text type was set in 11-point Caslon Pro.

To the young boys in my family,
from the East Coast of America to
the East Coast of Africa, I love you . . .
Saburi, Busaro, Juston, and Ames

Acknowledgments: As with *Safe at Home, Slam Dunk!* was
written with the support and encouragement of a number of
people. I'd like to give special thanks to my mother, Rachel
Robinson; my son, Jesse Simms; my editor, Sheila Keenan;
publicist Charisse Meloto; and the entire Scholastic family. I'd
also like to thank artist Kadir Nelson; the boys and girls from
Harlem RBI and from Simon Baruch Middle School 104; their
former principal, Margaret Struk; and parent Leo Stephens. To
all, I send my love and deep appreciation.

CHAPTER ONE

Jumper slammed his locker shut and raced to his homeroom. He slid into his seat just as the bell rang. It was his second week in the sixth grade at Langston Hughes Middle School, and his first day on time for all his classes.

There was no excuse for his being late. The Harlem brownstone he shared with his mother and grandmother was only a block from school. He just cut it too close; he'd have to do better.

"Elijah J. Breeze," Mrs. Miller called out.

Jumper lifted the index finger of his right hand. His teachers insisted on calling him Elijah; his friends knew him as Jumper.

There were advantages to being first on the attendance roll,

Jumper thought, as his mind wandered without fear of interruption. On this particular afternoon, Jumper's attention was on his after-school plans.

Mrs. Miller hammered out names with painstaking accuracy: Juston. Nico. Jabari. Lilli. Jamilla. Brooklyn. Francisco. Eddie. Quinsetta. Travor.

Homeroom was the first and last period of the day. Mrs. Miller used the time to keep her sixth graders organized. But even with Mrs. Miller's help, Jumper still found the day's rhythm confusing. He brought the wrong books to class and got lost in crowded hallways, amidst unfamiliar faces and languages. By the last period of the day, Jumper was ready to explode on the basketball court. Today was no different, except he would be shooting hoops at a store and mixing it with some NBA stars.

The dismissal bell rang. Jumper bolted out of the classroom, dodging other students, and burst out of the front door. He spotted his best friend, Kelvin Francis, waved, and ran toward him. He and Kelvin had met over the summer. They were both eleven, but Kelvin was six months older and Jumper was three inches taller.

"This has been the longest day!" Jumper complained as the boys knocked knuckles.

"It was hard to keep my mind on anything but basketball!" Kelvin said.

"I was so distracted that I bumped right into the kid with the blond streak in the front of his hair," Jumper said.

Kelvin laughed. "Eddie, right?"

"Yeah. He called me a complete nerd," Jumper reported.

Kelvin cracked up. "What'd you say?"

"I called him a loser!"

"Way to go, bro." Kelvin planted a high five on his friend. "Got to have a quick comeback. He's got a lot of nerve. Eddie's more of a nerd then you are. He owns a business!"

"Really?" Jumper said.

"Yeah. Designs these cool cards on his computer. They sell them in the bookstore on 125th Street. I know because he's in my art class and the teacher had him bring in some of his cards. Eddie says he makes enough money to buy his own clothes and video games. But you work at your grandmother's Laundromat for bucks. So, he doesn't have anything on you," Kelvin said.

"It's not the same. That's her business. Not mine."

"Anyway, don't let it get to you. Eddie's just messing with you 'cause you're so smart," Kelvin said.

"You're smart, too," Jumper reminded his friend.

"Yeah, but I'm not in any advanced placement classes. What's that they call you? Gifted?"

"So?"

"Well, that jumps the smart meter up a notch," Kelvin answered. "You're super smart *and* from Connecticut. In Harlem, that means double trouble," he teased.

"How long have I got to live in New York before people quit reminding me that I moved from Connecticut?"

"Not sure," Kelvin admitted. "You're my first friend from outside Harlem."

Jumper turned away and looked at the kids streaming out of school. Would New York kids ever *really* accept him? he wondered. "Come on, let's get out of here," he said. "I don't want to be late."

The boys headed toward the bus stop.

"It might rain," Jumper said, looking up at the clouds.

"So? The event's inside," Kelvin replied.

"I know. It's just that the bus moves even slower when it's raining."

"We could take the train," Kelvin suggested.

"No. I promised my mom that we'd stay above-ground," Jumper answered.

Still, the boys hesitated as they passed the entrance to the subway station. Jumper yanked Kelvin's sleeve. "No, man," Jumper said, remembering the time he'd told his mom that he was going to Kelvin's house, but went to the video arcade instead. That unauthorized change in plans, as his mother had called it, cost him two weeks of privileges. No, the bus was slow, but what they'd agreed on. "Let's keep it real. With basketball season almost here, I don't want to lose any privileges."

Jumper and Kelvin turned the corner and walked south on Eighth Avenue. They spotted the express bus a block away and broke into a trot.

The boys climbed aboard, flashed their student IDs, and made their way to empty seats. They shifted their backpacks off their shoulders and stuffed them on the floor.

As soon as the bus pulled away from the curb, Jumper checked his watch. The sporting goods store was in the heart of the city's business district, nearly seventy-five blocks away. He hoped they'd make it on time.

The bus rolled down Eighth Avenue, stopping to pick up passengers every five or ten blocks. He wished the new bunch of people boarding the bus would step on it.

"Still can't believe our luck," Jumper said.

"Me, neither," Kelvin replied.

"Have you ever won an essay contest before?" Jumper asked Kelvin.

"No. You?"

"Once. It was for our local newspaper back in my old town in Connecticut. You had to write an essay describing your neighborhood. I won a gift certificate to a sporting goods store. Got a new basketball out of that deal," Jumper told him.

"Cool. What did you write about this time?" Kelvin asked.

Jumper shifted uncomfortably in his seat. For some reason, it'd been easier to write about his father than to talk about him. "I wrote about how much my life has changed since my dad died," he finally said. "What about you?"

"Funny, I wrote about my dad, too," Kelvin replied.

"What'd you say?" Jumper asked.

"I wrote about the last time I was in St. Croix visiting

him. He took me to a basketball clinic run by Tim Duncan," Kelvin said.

"Tim Duncan, the basketball player?" Jumper asked.

"Of course."

"What was he doing in St. Croix?"

"He grew up there."

"Oh, yeah. I forgot."

"He's coming to New York soon," Kelvin added.

"Who? Tim Duncan?"

"No," Kelvin replied. "My dad."

"Gotcha. That'll be cool," Jumper said. "Do you know how many kids will be there today?" Jumper's mind was stuck on the upcoming basketball clinic.

"Should be twenty winners. Two students from ten New York City schools. At least, that's what my home-room teacher told me," Kelvin replied.

"That means we're the only kids representing Langston Hughes."

"I guess so," Kelvin said.

"Awesome. Hey, you think they'll throw in tickets to a Knicks game?" Jumper asked.

Kelvin lit up. "That would be hot!" Kelvin said. "Kinda wish we were going to the Garden," he added.

Jumper looked at his friend. "Me, too," he said, remembering the time his father had taken him to his first professional basketball game. New York played Detroit and blew them away. It was the most exciting night of his life. "I went there a couple of times."

"Yeah? What's it like?" Kelvin asked.

"Fun. Noisy. I saw Quentin hit a three-pointer once. Man, the fans jumped out of their seats so fast I almost got knocked two rows down," said Jumper.

"I know what you mean about crazy fans. It's like that at the Rucker. Folks go nuts!" Kelvin said.

"What's the Rucker?" Jumper asked.

"Oh, man, you never heard of the Rucker?" replied Kelvin.

Jumper shook his head. "No."

"Then you don't know nothin' about street ball," Kelvin told him.

"So tell me," Jumper prodded.

"The Rucker's a park in Harlem where big-name players come uptown to play local street stars, and record labels put together teams of rappers."

"Sweet!" said Jumper.

"Yeah. There are basketball tournaments in the summer. Can't hardly get into the Rucker because it's so crowded," Kelvin said, smiling. "Man, you've got to get with it. You want kids to stop messing with you, you've got to be in the know."

"So take me up there, then," Jumper suggested.

"Next summer," Kelvin replied.

"Next summer?" Jumper repeated. "Why not next week?"

"'Cause, like I said, the Rucker tournaments are in the summer. I once saw this high school kid go up against some NBA gods," Kelvin continued.

"Bet he got whipped," Jumper said.

"No way. He could take on the baddest players from the pros."

"So did he play ball in college?" Jumper asked.

"College?" Kelvin rolled his eyes.

"What about the pros? Did he get drafted?"

"It's not like that, man," Kelvin said slowly.

"What do you mean?"

"Just 'cause you can ball doesn't mean you'll get drafted," he replied.

"I know that," Jumper said. "I was just checking since you said he was so bad."

"I don't even know if the kid finished high school," Kelvin said.

"Now that's sad," Jumper said.

"Yeah, well. That's life on the streets," Kelvin replied, turning away.

The bus turned left at 110th Street and hugged the perimeter of Central Park. It was a mass of grass and trees, playfields, and ice-skating rinks sandwiched between tall, concrete buildings. Bikers raced to keep pace with yellow cabs and cars. Joggers hoofed it along the path surrounding the reservoir. A dog-walker was being dragged ten different ways by ten different dogs. Jumper jabbed Kelvin in the ribs and pointed. Both boys laughed.

The bus neared their stop. Jumper could feel the excitement. "I wonder if any of the Knicks players will show up with Patrick Ewing?" he asked.

"Isn't Patrick enough?" Kelvin asked.

"Sure, Patrick's a legend, but he's not playing basketball anymore. I'd like to see one of the young guys. Someone I watch on TV."

"Sweet," Kelvin muttered in awe as a black Porsche sped past the bus. "Hey," he said, nudging Jumper. "What kind of car do you think Patrick drives?"

Jumper shrugged his shoulders. "The man's seven feet tall! Not many cars he'll fit in," he said.

"You're right. Probably a Hummer," Kelvin suggested. "That's what I'm going to drive someday. I want a black one with windows so dark nobody will be able to see inside. Black on black. Yeah, baby. That's for me!"

"Man, you're going to be too short for a Hummer and too poor to pay for the gas," Jumper teased.

"No way! I'm gonna get rich playing ball for the Knicks," Kelvin said, sitting taller in his seat. "Besides, Hummers make you tall."

"Got no argument here," Jumper said. "But my mom told me Hummers are bad news for the environment."

"I don't know nothing about that," Kelvin replied, "and this is our stop."

The bus pulled over at the next corner; the two boys raced to the exit.

"Come on," Jumper said. "Patrick Ewing's waiting."

CHAPTER TWO

Jumper was still pumped the next morning. He floated through the halls oblivious to the noise, crowd, or his impending disgrace when the teacher discovered that he hadn't finished his reading homework. He slipped into the seat behind his friend Dakota, and poked her shoulder blade with his pencil.

"Quit it, Jumper!"

"He came!"

"Who came?"

"Patrick Ewing!"

Dakota frowned.

"Girls," Jumper murmured in disgust. "Seven-foot center. Used to play for the Knicks," he explained.

Dakota had been the pitcher on Jumper's team at last summer's baseball clinic. They had two things in common: Both of them had just moved to Harlem that summer, and they were different from most of the kids living there. Jumper was black and from suburban Connecticut. Dakota was white and had moved to Harlem from the Upper West Side.

"Nia was looking for you yesterday. She's got something important to tell you," Dakota said.

Jumper turned around and looked for Nia. She was another friend from summer baseball camp. Nia was too far away for him to mess with. She had her head deep inside a book. Jumper figured she hadn't finished the reading assignment, either. He turned back to Dakota. "What'd she want?"

"Think she'd tell me?" Dakota asked.

"You're friends, aren't you?" Jumper replied.

"Maybe," Dakota said.

Jumper was confused. The two girls had been friends all summer. "What are you talking about?" he asked.

"We're not speaking," Dakota told him.

"How come?"

"Well, Nia came over to my house when one of my

friends from 94th Street was visiting. Anyway, they got into it. Nia got mad at both of us and left. That's all," Dakota said.

Jumper just shook his head. He didn't bother asking what they argued about. Girls were always falling in and out of friendship. It was a stupid game boys didn't play. *They'll be best friends again tomorrow,* he thought.

Soon as class was dismissed, Jumper rushed over to Nia.

"I've got three minutes to get to class," he told her.

"Me, too," Nia replied.

"So, what's so important?" he asked.

Nia shrugged and flipped her head to the side.

"Don't play games, Nia. I've got to get to social studies."

"Didn't Dakota tell you?" Nia asked.

"No, she said to ask you."

"Marcus is here. You might run into him," Nia said, then turned and started to walk away.

"Nia!" Jumper shouted.

She looked back and smiled sweetly. "Yes?"

"What are you talking about?"

Nia stopped walking. "Oh, all right," she said, and turned to face Jumper. "Marcus will be at Langston starting Monday. He's here today meeting with the principal," she reported.

"Marcus, here?" Jumper felt sick to his stomach. Marcus was Nia's older brother. He liked to play the role of tough guy. Marcus had given him plenty of trouble during baseball camp. He was the team captain and not patient with Jumper's beginning baseball skills. They'd finally worked things out well enough that their team won, but Jumper wasn't happy about coming face-to-face with Marcus again.

"Yeah. And, he's not happy 'bout it, either," Nia said.

"What happened? I thought he was going to some Catholic school," Jumper asked.

"Got kicked out," Nia said. "Can we discuss this later?"

Jumper's stomach tightened. Marcus was coming to Langston. That wasn't good news. And what had he done to get kicked out of school, anyway? How would he act when they ran into each other? Would just the sight of Jumper make him mad? Would he try to push him around? Call him names? Make his life miserable? Or had they really settled their differences at baseball camp?

"Meet me and Kelvin in front of school soon as it lets out," Jumper called out.

Nia spun around and shoved a finger in Jumper's face. "Don't be ordering me around, Elijah J. Breeze."

Oops, he'd pushed too far. Jumper pressed on to his next class, mad with himself. Now he'd blown it with Nia and would have to be even more careful with her brother. Jumper slipped into social studies seconds before the bell. But his mind wasn't on history; he was too busy worrying. Did you ever stop being afraid of a bully?

CHAPTER THREE

Marcus stayed on Jumper's mind. He tossed most of the night. His big fear was that Marcus would embarrass him in front of his classmates.

The next morning, Jumper arrived at school early. He had to get to school ahead of everyone else and establish his turf. As Jumper burst through the front door thirty minutes before school officially opened, he bumped into the security guard.

Jumper swallowed hard. Mr. Wright was a big man with large hands and a deep voice. "Uh, good morning, Mr. Wright," he said, staring up into the security guard's stern face.

Tyrone Wright was Langston Hughes's answer to

school security. From his desk just inside the front door, Mr. Wright controlled visitors and students alike. He knew most of the kids by name and was often heard calling some student out for wearing pants too low, using curse words, or pushing some kid around. "This isn't elementary school!" he'd boom.

"Elijah Breeze," Mr. Wright greeted him. "Early morning, huh?"

"Uh, I wanted to shoot some hoops," Jumper replied.

Mr. Wright checked his watch. "You've got ten minutes before the school yard's open," he bellowed.

"By the time I drop my books at my locker and get outside, ten minutes should be up," Jumper said hopefully. He didn't want Mr. Wright to upset his plans.

Mr. Wright smiled. "I'll get Mr. Saunders to cover the door and I'll meet you at the courts."

"But . . . but . . ." Jumper stammered.

"Ten minutes. Man-to-man," he said, meeting Jumper's startled gaze squarely.

"Yes, sir."

"Mr. Wright's good enough," Tyrone called back as he headed off to find Mr. Saunders.

Jumper pulled his basketball out of his locker, tossed his backpack in, and kicked the door shut. His plan definitely hadn't included playing ball with Mr. Wright. Jumper bounced the ball nervously. Mr. Wright might scare the kids off. Maybe Marcus wouldn't come near the courts. Sighing, he put his concerns aside and headed to the yard.

Mr. Wright was waiting for him. "Jumper," he said tentatively. "Mind if I call you that?"

"Okay by me," Jumper replied.

"I'm glad that you came in early today," Tyrone Wright began.

"Why's that?" Jumper asked.

"Coach Coleman and I are good friends," he replied.

"Oh," Jumper said. Coach Coleman had run the baseball camp that Jumper attended over the summer. All the kids liked him. Coach Coleman was the one who had forced Jumper and Marcus to work as a team.

"Coach and I, we talk. Sorry to hear about your dad," he said.

"Thanks," Jumper said.

"He told me that you and Marcus got into it this summer," Mr. Wright said.

Jumper laughed. "You could say that. Coach helped us work some things out, though."

"How'd that go?" Mr. Wright asked.

"All right."

"So you're okay with Marcus coming to Langston?"

"Doesn't bother me," Jumper lied.

"Good. I'll have no trouble out of you and Marcus, right?"

"Hopefully not," said Jumper, "but you'll have to talk with Marcus."

"I plan to do just that. But if there's trouble, I'll hear about it. I'll be on you two like glue. So don't start anything and don't get into it with Marcus if he starts something. A fight takes two, remember," Mr. Wright warned.

"Don't worry about me," Jumper said.

"I worry about all of the students at Langston. It's my job. I'm here if you need me," Mr. Wright said, passing the ball to Jumper. He took a shot. Mr. Wright grabbed the rebound and sank the ball through the hoop. "Do you like Langston?"

"It's all right," Jumper replied, taking control of the ball and holding it against his chest. "No basketball team, though. That's a problem for me." He bounced the ball a few times just to remind Mr. Wright why they were outside.

"I intend to do something about that," Mr. Wright stated.

"But I thought the gym floor was messed up. Can't have a basketball program outside," Jumper said.

"Don't worry. We'll get the floor fixed."

"In time for this season? In time to start up a team?" Jumper asked.

"I'm working on it. I plan to coach the boys' team. The principal's trying to get someone to organize the girls. Could use your help spreading the word."

"All right," Jumper agreed.

"Bring your friends by the library tomorrow. We're having our first meeting to discuss the basketball program," Mr. Wright said.

"What time?" Jumper asked.

"Three fifteen."

"Now let's see what you've got." Mr. Wright stole the ball from Jumper, passed it back, and watched how he handled the ball.

Jumper moved smoothly, switching hands as he drove to the basket for a jump shot. A few feet from the basket, he squared his body and jumped into the air with his arms raised. Jumper pushed the basketball with his right hand, flicked his wrist, released the ball, and landed on bent knees.

Swish! The basketball sank into the basket without even touching the rim.

Jumper quickly retrieved the ball and dribbled around Mr. Wright, challenging him into a defensive stance.

"Quit topping the ball," warned Mr. Wright.

Jumper readjusted his grip. He faked the security guard out by quickly shifting direction and lost him for a few seconds. Jumper went up for a layup, but missed. The ball bounced off the backboard and into Mr. Wright's powerful hands.

Dribble. Dribble. Drive. Jump. *Swish!*

They didn't keep score, but Jumper knew that he had proved to be a tough opponent. Feeling confident, he attempted a three-pointer from mid-court: *swish!*

Mr. Wright grabbed the rebound and dodged Jumper. He came around from behind, lifted for a clean shot, and fired. Jumper flew into the air, arms high above his head. He snatched the ball out of the air and successfully blocked Mr. Wright's shot. Jumper landed, twisted, and fired. The ball sank through the net.

"Nice shot," Mr. Wright called. He grabbed the rebound and sent the ball up and through the hoop.

They played on before a gathering crowd. Jumper hoped that Marcus was outside and watching him.

"Man, you gonna let that kid outshoot you?" one of the boys shouted to Mr. Wright.

"Come and give me some help!" Mr. Wright replied.

"Not *me*, man. I'd rather watch you get slaughtered," another boy yelled back.

"Your choice." The security guard dunked the ball.

"Sweet!" someone called from the sidelines.

Jumper grabbed the ball and shot from mid-court. *Swish!* A self-satisfied smile spread across his face. He *was* good!

Their game was interrupted by the sound of the warning bell. It was a reminder that first period began in ten minutes.

Mr. Wright extended his right hand to Jumper. "Nice job," he said, slapping him a high five. "See you tomorrow."

Jumper nodded toward Mr. Wright. When he turned, Jumper faced several of the older boys. The boys parted and Marcus stepped forward.

Jumper met Marcus's gaze squarely. "Welcome to Langston Hughes," he said, grinning.

CHAPTER FOUR

When Nia heard that Mr. Wright was organizing the boys, she rounded up her friends. They huddled outside the library, plotting their next move.

"I heard that Mr. Wright is starting a boys' basketball team," Nia told the girls.

"The security guard?" Sabrina asked.

"Yeah. He's going to be the coach," Nia said.

"Without a gym?" Dakota questioned.

"I guess," Nia said.

"Who's coaching the girls?" Lilli wanted to know.

Nia held up her hands. "I don't have any answers," she said. "That's why we've got to bust into the meeting."

"You mean we're not invited?" Dakota asked.

"That's right. The meeting's just for boys," Nia said.

"Oh, that's not good!" Lilli said.

"I agree," Dakota chimed in.

"We want to play basketball for Langston Hughes, too," Sabrina added.

"What if Mr. Wright says there'll be no girls' team?" Dakota asked.

Nia pouted. She kicked the wall with her sneaker. "We'll tell him that it's unfair. Can't just be boys representing Langston," Nia said. She liked competing.

"Yeah. We've got to have a girls' team to play other schools. Besides, we can show the boys just how bad we are," Sabrina added.

"Is that what this is about?" Dakota asked. "Showing up the boys?"

"No," Nia declared. "It's about our rights!"

Sabrina frowned. "Rights?"

"Girls deserve a team, too!" Nia said. "We've got to make our point! Come on. Let's go make it happen."

Nia charged through the door to the library and headed for the back room where the meeting was being held. When she reached it, Nia put on the brakes so quickly that Sabrina and Dakota bumped into her.

Tyrone Wright looked up. A dozen boys turned their heads as well.

"Yes, Nia?" said Mr. Wright.

"May we come in?" Nia asked politely.

"Of course," Mr. Wright answered.

The girls entered and walked up to the front of the room.

"What's on your minds, girls?"

"We heard that you were starting a basketball program," Lilli said.

"We're talking about that now," Mr. Wright admitted.

"Just for boys?" Dakota asked.

Mr. Wright laced his long fingers together and looked directly at the girls. "And you object, right?"

"That's right, Mr. Wright. It's not fair to do for the boys and not the girls," Nia complained.

"Yeah. It's not fair," Sabrina added.

"Mr. Wright, we just want to play basketball, too," Dakota stated firmly.

"That's right. Can't just be boys representing Langston," Nia insisted.

"Give it a rest, Nia," Jumper warned.

Nia whipped around. Fisted hands on her hips, she glared angrily at Jumper. "*You* give it a rest! We want a girls' basketball team! Period!" Nia fired back at Jumper.

"Yeah, we kicked butt in baseball and wait until you see us tear down the court. Nia may be short, but she can jump higher than you, *Jumper*!" Sabrina said.

"I *doubt* that," Jumper said sarcastically. No girl could outjump him.

"Oh, really? I'll show you!" Nia challenged.

Kelvin stepped between Nia and Jumper and pointed a finger in Nia's face. "We're sick of bossy girls," he spat.

"Enough!" Mr. Wright shouted. "Let's start from the beginning, okay?" he continued. "There will be two teams representing Langston Hughes. One for the boys and one for the girls. Principal Young expects to have a coach for the girls very soon.

"I'm sorry this wasn't settled before meeting with the boys. They were just ready to get going and so was I. When I leave here I'm going straight to Principal Young to check up on your coach. Enough said."

Mr. Wright turned back to the boys. "Our first practice is next Tuesday. We'll meet on the yard at three fifteen sharp! Thanks for coming today . . . all of you."

Nia, Sabrina, Lilli, and Dakota left without saying anything more to the boys. Outside, they regrouped.

"Are you all right with what Mr. Wright said?" Dakota asked.

"Just as long as we get a team," Nia replied. "But I'm still glad we showed up today. If we hadn't, Mr. Wright wouldn't push the principal," Nia said.

"Got that right," Sabrina added.

"Hey, want to come over to my house tomorrow?" Dakota asked her friends.

"I'll have to check with my mother," Sabrina said.

"Oh, yeah. I forgot about your little brother. Do you still have to pick him up after school?" Dakota asked.

"No. He's in nursery school now, so my mom picks him up after work. I'll let you know in the morning," Sabrina replied.

"Is your friend coming?" Nia asked.

"Which friend?"

"You know, the one who was afraid of all the black people in the park," Nia reminded Dakota.

"Oh, that. No, she's not coming."

"What are you talking about?" Sabrina asked.

"Dakota has this friend from her old neighborhood who's afraid of Harlem," Nia said.

"Nia, give her a break," Dakota defended.

"Do I know who you're talking about?" Sabrina asked.

"No," Dakota said.

"Well, tell me what's going on!"

"My friend Annie came up to my house. Nia was over and suggested that we go to the park. Annie said she didn't want to go outside, that's all," Dakota said.

"Because there were too many black people," Nia corrected Dakota.

"Well, it's not so easy fitting in when you're the only white person," Dakota said.

"You don't seem to have any problems," Sabrina said.

"It's different with me."

"Why's that?" Nia asked.

"I've been to baseball camp and . . ." Dakota hesitated. "I like living in Harlem. I have friends. I like my school, but my sister's not happy. She still goes to a private school in our old neighborhood. All her friends are from down there."

"I hear you. I once went to a sleepover camp and I was the only black girl. I felt funny. The first night I called my mom and told her to come and get me. She told me that I'd have to stick it out. It worked. I got used to the camp and made plenty of friends," Sabrina said.

"Well, I feel strange in my own house," Nia said.

Sabrina and Dakota stared at her.

"Things are so bad with Marcus and my dad that I hate going home," she continued.

"How bad?" Sabrina asked. She'd spent time at Nia's house and knew that her parents were always yelling.

"Dad's furious that Marcus got kicked out of Catholic school. He wants to send him away to a military school! Can you imagine Marcus taking orders from some officer?"

"Well, maybe it will be good for him," Dakota suggested.

"Marcus doesn't want to go," Nia said. "Anyway, I hate going home."

"Maybe it would be better for everyone if Marcus did go away to school," Sabrina said, agreeing with Dakota.

"Who knows," Nia said, slumping down to the floor and leaning against her locker. "I'm hoping that he'll like Langston Hughes and start to do better."

"Maybe you should talk with Mr. Wright. You know, ask him to look out for Marcus," Sabrina suggested.

"I could," Nia said.

"Or you could talk with Jumper," Dakota suggested.

"What for? He and Marcus hardly get along," Nia reminded her.

"I bet if you let Jumper know how bad things are for Marcus, he'd know what to do," Dakota insisted. "Jumper always has good ideas. Maybe it's something simple like asking Marcus to join the boys' basketball team."

Nia thought for a moment. "That's a pretty good idea. It just might work." She got up from the floor. "Thanks, guys," she said, then looked directly at Dakota. "Your house. Tomorrow. See ya." Then Nia hurried off to look for Jumper.

Nia found him shooting baskets on the school yard. "Hey," she called.

Jumper turned around and waved. "Where are your sneakers?" he yelled back.

Nia looked down at her shoes and smiled. Jumper had just invited her to play basketball. "Can't play today. I've got things to do, but thanks for asking," she said.

"What're you doing here, then?" Jumper asked.

"I came looking for you. I need to ask you a favor," Nia replied.

"If it's about the basketball program, I don't have any-thing else to say. It's up to Principal Young and Mr. Wright."

"I know. And I'm cool with that as long as the girls don't have to wait a long time for a coach."

"Then what's up?" Jumper asked.

"It's Marcus," Nia said.

"What about him?" Jumper asked.

"I have no right to ask, but I need your help."

"With Marcus?"

"Yeah. I'm worried about him. Things between him and my dad are really bad. If Marcus doesn't do good at Langston, he'll probably be sent away to military school. He wants to stay home, be near his friends . . . you know? Think you could invite him to join the basket-ball team?" Nia asked.

"If I ask him, he may not join," Jumper replied.

"He will. Marcus loves basketball."

"No problem, then," Jumper said.

"Thanks. I owe you one."

"No, you don't. Nothing owed. We're friends, Nia, remember?" Jumper said.

"And friends stick together — fight, too. You know, I think this could make the difference," she replied.

"What do you mean?"

"Marcus didn't play any sports at his old school," Nia said.

"You never did tell me what happened with that," Jumper reminded Nia.

"You better leave that alone."

"Why?" Jumper persisted.

"Marcus doesn't like anybody in his business," she whispered as her brother approached them.

"Did I hear my name?" Marcus asked.

Jumper spun around. "I was just wondering if you're planning on joining the basketball team," he said.

"Didn't know anything about it," Marcus replied.

"Mr. Wright — you know, the security guard — he's starting a boys' basketball program. We'll have to practice out here on the yard until the gym floor's fixed."

"Out here?" Marcus asked, kicking stones with his sneakers. "This ground's not even level. Can't be much of a program."

"Mr. Wright says the gym will be ready soon," Jumper assured him.

"No girls on the team, right?" Marcus asked, glancing over at his sister.

Nia boiled, but kept her mouth shut. She could see that her plan was working.

"The girls will have their own team," Jumper said.

"I'll give it a go," Marcus replied.

"Cool. Our first practice is next Tuesday at three fifteen."

Marcus grabbed Jumper's basketball and took a shot. As it sank through the hoop he growled, "Stay out of my business!"

CHAPTER FIVE

Monday morning was reserved for a weekly sixth-grade assembly, but Principal Young called a special meeting.

"Good morning," she greeted two hundred and fifty eager sixth graders. "Thank you for settling down so quickly. We have important business today. I'll start with sports at Langston Hughes. As you know, our gym had a flood last year and we had to suspend our indoor physical education program. Well, I'm happy to announce that we intend on having it fully operational for the basketball season. And Mr. Wright and Miss King will coach the boys' and girls' basketball teams! Let's give them some loud applause!"

The students cheered and clapped at the news until Principal Young signaled for quiet.

"Secondly, I'm pleased to announce that it's time for student council elections. We'll devote two weeks to the election of this year's student government.

"The student council elections serve as a model civics lesson. They provide students with a voice in how the school is run. Each grade will elect a class representative. All of you will be involved in the process. For the next week, in each of your classes you'll study some aspect of campaigning and the political process. In art, you'll design posters for the candidates. In social studies, you'll study the current presidential campaign. In English, you'll learn to write a persuasive paper and practice public speaking. The second week, candidates will campaign. It's going to be hard work, but fun, too!

"Everyone is welcome and encouraged to run for office, but all candidates must register and meet with me. So mark your calendars! October first is election day at Langston Hughes Middle School!"

After fielding questions, Principal Young dismissed the students for lunch. Once inside the cafeteria, discussions on the student council elections continued.

Jumper, Kelvin, Nia, Dakota, Sabrina, Juston, Eddie,

Lilli, and Callie grabbed lunch and sat together so that they could discuss the student council itself.

Jumper tossed down his cold chicken pattie on stale bread in disgust. "If I were class representative, I'd get better food into this cafeteria," he grumbled.

"Yeah, even the French fries taste like they were cooked yesterday and then reheated in the microwave until they were hard," Dakota added.

"Student council's a joke," Juston threw in.

"Why do you say that?" Nia asked.

"It's a bunch of nerds sitting around talking. Nothing changes," Juston complained.

"Depends who wins," Kelvin said.

"Are you interested in running?" Lilli asked.

"Only if I didn't have to go to any meetings," Kelvin teased.

"Come on. It's not that much work," Sabrina said.

"It'll look good on a college application," Eddie told them.

"Man, you're crazy. Like they care what you did in sixth grade," Juston said.

"Hey, can we get back to the elections?" Nia cut in.

"What exactly does a student council representative do?" Eddie asked.

"They find out what sixth graders want and then tell the other people on the student council," Kelvin told the group.

"Yeah, and since sixth graders are at the bottom of all the students, nobody cares what they want," Sabrina said.

"We need someone who will make them listen," Callie said.

"Someone who's a leader," Eddie suggested.

Jumper did a quick self-evaluation. When he was in Connecticut, he'd organized his friends and they'd started a landscaping business for neighbors. Well, "business" was a stretch, but they had raked leaves and bagged them. He was a pretty good listener. Hadn't he just listened to Nia and done what she'd asked him to do? And, last summer, he'd stepped into the role of co-captain for their baseball team and done pretty well. He was a leader.

"Anyone interested in running?" Kelvin asked.

No one spoke up.

"It's just a popularity contest," Sabrina suggested.

"Yeah, the person who has the most friends wins," Nia said.

"Except most of the sixth grade class come from different schools," Jumper reminded her. "I'd like to run," he admitted.

"What! You came from a whole different *state*. Nobody knows you," Nia replied.

"If he runs, people will get to know him," Kelvin suggested.

"It would be a good way for me to meet kids, I guess," Jumper said.

"Why don't you have a party instead?" asked Nia.

"Very funny, but maybe Nia has a point," Jumper said. "This is my first time going to a public school in New York. I've only lived in Harlem a few months. I wouldn't win."

"You could. In two weeks, the whole school will know your name. We just have to figure out how," Kelvin told him.

"I don't know all the issues," Jumper continued.

"Who does?" Dakota shrugged. "We're all new to this school and not all the students live in Harlem. So, I don't buy Nia's point."

"So, his slogan's what? Vote for Jumper and vote for a basketball program?" Nia asked sarcastically.

"I think Jumper should run," Kelvin pushed. "He's got lots of good ideas. He's a good friend. He works hard. And he's smart."

"I agree," Juston said.

"Hold up!" Nia broke in. "There are other people at this table who may want to run. Like me," she admitted. "I've got good ideas, too! Plus I'd have a better chance of winning."

"That's right!" Dakota threw in her support.

"I know plenty of kids already. I've lived in this neighborhood all my life. I went to elementary school down the street. And I've got a big mouth," Nia insisted.

"You've got that right. And we're all tired of hearing you complain!" Eddie said.

Nia stood up, mad. "Get used to it, because I'm running!"

"So am I!" Jumper declared.

"I'll be Jumper's campaign manager," Kelvin offered.

Dakota tossed Sabrina a quick glance. "Nia, Sabrina and I will help you," Dakota said.

Callie and Lilli threw their support to Nia and the party lines were drawn: boys against girls.

"Then let's get started," Nia said.

The girls got up from the table and headed out of the cafeteria.

"See you on the campaign trail," Nia called back.

The word spread quickly. By three fifteen, students were filing out of school talking about the elections. Kelvin, Jumper, Juston, and Eddie didn't stop to join in the talk. They were on a mission. Jumper wanted to tell his grandmother and start planning his campaign. With his boys at his side, he charged down the front steps, heading to Miss BB's Laundromat.

"What will she say?" Kelvin asked.

"She'll be happy," Jumper said with confidence. "Of course, she and my mom will say that I've got to keep up my grades. That's what they said when I told them about the basketball team."

"Would you give up basketball?" Juston asked.

"You crazy!" Jumper replied.

"No. That's not happening. You'll have to do both *and* keep up with your grades. You can handle it, man. You're super smart, remember?" Kelvin said.

Jumper laughed and plowed through the doors to the Laundromat. He crossed the room and planted a loud, wet kiss on his grandmother's cheek.

"Boy!" she scolded, pulling back. "I told you about those wet kisses. You must want something," Miss BB fussed. She adored her grandson and was always happy to see him and his friends.

"Hi, Miss BB!" Kelvin greeted her with a firm handshake like he'd been taught.

"Grandma, I'd like you to meet my friends Juston and Eddie."

"Nice to meet you," she said, shaking the boys' hands before turning to Jumper. "What are you kids up to? Or did you come to work and make a few dollars?"

Jumper laughed. "Not today, Grandma. We wanted to talk with you about something."

"Well, come on in my office. I've got a few minutes before those dryers are done."

The boys followed Miss BB into her small office. Jumper sat on the edge of the desk; the others sat in chairs or slumped to the floor.

"Must be serious," she said. "We could be here a while. Should I order chicken from next door?"

"Mmm. I'm starving!" Jumper said first.

"So are we," Kelvin, Eddie, and Juston chimed in.

"Let me make a quick call. Wings okay?"

"Sure!"

Miss BB ordered two dozen wings with a side of hot sauce and fries. She settled back in her chair, ready to hear them out.

"Grandma, we're going to have student council elections at Langston," Jumper began. "We have a week to get set up and a week to campaign. Elections will be October first and I'm running for sixth-grade representative," he told her.

Miss BB burst out of her seat. "Son, that's the best news I've heard in a long time!" She grabbed Jumper and smothered him in her arms. "You'll be a wonderful representative. Couldn't do no better than you. Who else is running?" she asked.

"Nia," Jumper replied.

"And there's only one representative from each class?" Miss BB asked.

"That's right."

"Well, that's okay. You can still be friends and compete against each other. Just as long as you talk it out. It's not that much different from baseball camp. You played on opposite teams, but still became friends. Well, you're both doing what's best for your school. Whoever wins will be a good representative."

"Told you so," Kelvin said.

"Kelvin's my campaign manager," Jumper told Miss BB.

"Good choice," Miss BB replied, smiling. "What about Juston and Eddie?"

"I'm in charge of entertainment," Juston said.

"I've got posters, flyers, and the Internet covered," Eddie added.

"Well, then you've got a great candidate and a highly skilled team. Your mom and I will supply food and behind-the-scenes cheerleading," she said with a chuckle. "Just give Nia a call, okay?"

Jumper gave his grandma's words some thought. "I guess you're right. I'll call Nia tonight and talk about it."

Kelvin slapped Jumper a high five.

"One other thing," Miss BB said.

"What's that?"

"You better bring home no less than a B-plus," his grandmother added. "I'm not having no excuses 'bout how much campaigning work you've got to do. It's a big responsibility, this student council, but you can do it, Elijah. I just know you can! Oops, my dryers just went off. You kids go out there and empty them for me," she instructed.

"Of course," they shouted, and rushed out to empty the dryers.

"Fold the clothes, too, while you're out there. Chicken will be here by the time you finish your work," Miss BB said with a chuckle. "I'm real proud of you, boy," she called out as Jumper looked back.

"Thanks, Grandma. Think Mom will agree?" he asked.

"Know she will. She'll be so happy. It means you're settling in and that's so important to her. Now get to work. I don't want the clothes to cool off. They start to wrinkle if they do. Mind the others. You know how I like my clothes folded," she added.

The boys folded clothes and started planning.

"What do we do first?" Jumper asked.

Heads turned to Kelvin.

"Come up with a slogan, I guess?" he replied tentatively. "My mom works for a politician. Sometimes I go with her to meetings. They're always coming up with slogans," Kelvin added.

"Okay. Then we'll come up with a slogan," Jumper said.

"We could make the flyers and posters," Eddie suggested.

"But we still need a slogan. Something funny," Kelvin added.

"I agree. Kids think you're all about the grades," Eddie said. "I sure did 'til I saw you hooping it up with the security guard," Eddie said.

"I remember," said Jumper. "Called me a complete nerd just 'cause I bumped into you in the hall. You're lucky I'm speaking to you," he teased.

"You're lucky to have me on your team!" Eddie shot back.

"Eddie's right, you know," Kelvin said to Jumper. "You've said so yourself. I'd say that's an image problem that needs fixing. I mean it's good to be smart, but you're more than that. We've just got to let the kids know that while you're all about business, you can be fun, too!"

"According to you guys, I need to be an A-plus clown," Jumper joked.

They all laughed.

"Can we get back to the slogan?" Kelvin asked.

"I have an idea," Juston said, dropping the towel he was folding onto the table. "You could run a campaign about getting things done in the school and then add something silly like a thirty-minute joke period once a week."

Kelvin slapped Juston a high five. "You're good!" he complimented him.

"Do I have to make a speech?" Jumper asked.

"Yeah, but keep it fun," Kelvin replied.

"And you need to give away something cool," Juston suggested.

"Or good to eat . . . like candy or something," Eddie added.

"Isn't that a bribe?" Jumper asked.

"Sort of," Kelvin replied.

"It's a lot to do," Jumper said.

"Sure is," Juston agreed.

"It'll be over in two weeks," Kelvin reminded him.

"And after campaigning, it's easy," Eddie added.

"I doubt that," Jumper said.

"You kids stop talking and fold!" Miss BB shouted from the doorway.

They stopped talking and concentrated on folding clothes. Jumper tried to come up with a slogan, but all he could come up with were words from rap songs.

By now the boys were hungry, so they worked fast.

They had just finished when a delivery man walked into the Laundromat with a large, greasy-looking brown paper bag.

"Food's here!" Jumper cried.

Miss BB came out of her office to inspect the neatly folded clothes in their metal baskets. "Good job," she complimented the boys.

They wolfed down the chicken and raced off to the basketball courts for a quick game.

Kelvin and Eddie took on Jumper and Juston.

Eddie got the ball first and dribbled toward the basket. Juston lightly defended when he went up for a layup. The ball hit the backboard and fell through the hoop.

"Nice," Kelvin called out as he lifted into the air and snatched the ball before it hit the asphalt.

"Nice rebound," Juston shot back.

Jumper took possession of the ball. Kelvin and Eddie double-teamed him. Jumper dodged them with a well-executed fake, squared his long lean body with the basket, lifted straight up, and took his shot at the top of his jump. The ball swished through the basket as he landed in the same spot from which he'd taken the jump.

Juston stopped short. "Sweet!" he called out in true admiration.

"Guess you earned your nickname!" Kelvin praised his buddy.

"Speaking of nicknames, what name will you campaign under?" Eddie asked.

Jumper held the ball to his chest. He looked to Kelvin for an answer.

"Jumper," Kelvin replied confidently. "That way we'll keep it light."

"Fine with me," Jumper said.

"Good plan," Eddie chimed in.

"I've got it!" Kelvin sang out.

"Got what?" Jumper asked.

"Your slogan," Kelvin replied. *Jump up for Jumper!*

CHAPTER SIX

Mr. Wright blew the whistle, signaling the start of basketball practice.

"Okay, we'll start off slow, warm up, then practice jump shots," Mr. Wright said as the boys began practice. He motioned for the boys to stand in front of him. "When I say ten, raise both hands high into the air," Mr. Wright instructed.

Marcus shot Jumper a look of disgust. "Some basketball program," he muttered.

"Excuse me, Mr. Wright," Jumper called out.

"Yes, Jumper?"

"Uh, what do we call you?"

"Good question. On the court, call me Coach Wright.

Inside that building," he said, pointing to the school, "call me Mr. Wright. Got it?"

"Yes, sir — I mean, Coach Wright," Jumper replied.

"Okay. Let's get going. Ten!" Coach Wright shouted, catching Jumper and Marcus by surprise. They missed the first command. Jumper ignored Marcus and instead focused on Mr. Wright.

A few seconds passed. "Ten!" Coach Wright shouted as Jumper and Marcus threw their hands into the air.

"Ten!" Mr. Wright yelled again.

"Hey, Coach. This is hard!" Juston shouted.

"Ten!" Coach Wright shouted again without replying. Seconds passed.

"Ten!"

The boys burst out laughing as they reached for the sky.

"Good job!" Coach Wright finally called out. "Seemed like a silly game at first, right?"

Heads bobbed.

"Can anyone tell me what skill we just worked on?"

"Reflexes," Kelvin called out.

"Timing," Eddie offered.

"Listening," Jumper suggested.

"Correct. The first thing you need to learn is to listen to me. Understand?"

"Yes, Coach," Marcus shouted along with the others.

"When I blow the whistle, I expect silence. Agreed?"

"Yes, Coach Wright," they yelled out.

"We're here to build a strong team. That means working hard together. So what's our goal?" he asked the boys.

"To get a gym!" Jumper yelled out.

"I hear you, but what else are we working for?"

"To win!" Jumper said.

"To have fun!" Juston shouted.

"To play our best!" called another guy.

"And how do we reach our goal?" Coach Wright asked.

"Good attitude," Eddie volunteered.

"Lots of practice," Kelvin called out.

"Wanting it badly," Juston yelled.

"Hustle," Marcus added.

Coach Wright blew his whistle. "Okay. After we warm up, we'll move on to shooting," he said. "Layups, then jump shots.

"Hands over your heads!" Coach Wright yelled.

"Quick jumps!"

"Right leg!"

The boys counted along with their coach. "One, two, three, four, five . . ."

"Left leg!"

The boys quickly put their right legs down, lifted bent knees into the air, and started the count again. Some kids tripped and collided into one another. Laughter broke out.

Coach Wright didn't stop. "Right leg!" Most of the boys switched on cue. Others took a few seconds to get into rhythm.

"Nice job," the coach said finally. "Now that your arms and legs are warmed up, we'll spend the next twenty minutes on shooting. Let's go over the basics. Everyone wants to skip right to the jump shot, but first you have to master the layup. There's a rhythm to each shot. Dribble to the basket; step with your right leg; left leg down; drive your right knee into the air and lift off with the left; jump up; extend ball; shoot."

Practice was slow and deliberate. The more experienced players like Jumper, Marcus, and Kelvin had to help out with the less skilled boys. But when it was time for the jump shot, Jumper and Marcus showed off to loud cheers from the group.

"Drive, jump, swish," Coach Wright repeated as Jumper drove to the basket, jumped high into the air, and made his basket. The boys cheered one another on, regardless of whether or not the ball sailed through the net.

After practice, Jumper was stuffing his basketball into his backpack when he noticed a man walking toward him.

"Hey, Kelvin, check out that man," he whispered.

Kelvin turned his head. "Dad!" he shouted.

Jumper watched Kelvin leap into the man's arms, feeling a little left out. Until now, Kelvin's dad had been a mystery man.

"Told you I'd come," Mr. Francis said.

"When'd you get in?" Kelvin asked his father.

"I arrived in New York last night. I'm staying with my brother. When I called your mom this morning, she told me about practice." He paused, looking his son over. "You've grown a few inches."

"Yeah. Dad, this is my best friend, Elijah Breeze. We call him Jumper," Kelvin said.

"Nice to meet you, Elijah." Mr. Francis shook Jumper's hand.

"You, too, Mr. Francis," Jumper said. "It's okay if you call me Jumper, too."

"Works for me, Jumper," he replied, smiling.

"Come on, Dad, I want you to meet Coach Wright," Kelvin said.

They crossed the court and Kelvin made the introductions.

"Thanks for coming out today. I like parents to come to practice and see how hard we work," Coach Wright said.

"My father came all the way from St. Croix to see me," Kelvin told Coach Wright.

"St. Croix? I'm not familiar with it."

"It's one of the U.S. Virgin Islands," Mr. Francis told him. "My name's Kelvin, like my son."

"I'm Tyrone Wright. The kids call me Coach Wright out here, but inside I'm Mr. Wright in charge of security. Anyway, nice to meet you. I know Kelvin will be happy to have you around."

"He's grown," Mr. Francis replied proudly. "Looked good on the courts, too. All the boys did. When it gets cold, do you take practice inside?"

"That's the plan, but first we've got to repair the gym," Coach Wright replied.

"Oh. What needs to be done?" Mr. Francis asked.

"Our gym floor was ruined in a flood last year. We

need someone to lay a new one down. That takes money. We've raised most of the money we need, but we're still short some," Coach Wright told him.

"I just finished a big job in one of the high schools back home," Mr. Francis said.

"Are you a builder?"

"That's right. General contractor, really."

"Wow, you're my first parent with any real construction experience. Sure wish we could get you to help us out," Coach Wright said.

"I might be able to work something out," Mr. Francis said.

Jumper nudged Kelvin. They high-fived.

"I'd be happy to take a look at the gym and give you some idea about time and money," Mr. Francis offered.

"Got a few minutes?"

Mr. Francis nodded.

"Let's go."

The boys trailed behind the men.

"I thought your father was a fisherman?"

Kelvin laughed. "He likes to fish. That's how we spend our time when I'm down there. We even sell the fish, but he's got his own construction company."

"Oh," Jumper replied.

When they reached the gym, Coach Wright flicked on the lights. "Here we are," he said.

"It's cool having your dad here," Jumper whispered.

"I know. Wish he could stay forever," Kelvin replied. "He's kind of flaky. I hope he stays long enough to finish the floor."

"If he agrees to fix the gym, he'll be around for a while," Jumper said.

"Then we need to get him to say yes," Kelvin said.

They moved closer to the men so they could hear their conversation. After walking around the buckling floor, Mr. Francis and Coach Wright stopped to discuss the project in more detail.

"I'll do the work," Mr. Francis told Coach Wright.

Kelvin looked at Jumper and smiled.

"Really? You'll give me an estimate, then?"

"There's no charge for labor," Mr. Francis replied.

"That's amazing! What about a crew?"

"I'll get my brother to help. He's a master at this. We'll get one other man. That should do it. Once we get started, it shouldn't take more than a few weeks."

"Great!" Coach Wright clapped his hands.

"Yeah!" the boys shouted.

"Does that mean we'll be ready for the season?" Jumper asked.

"I think so," Coach Wright replied. "We're almost there. A fund-raiser would bring us over the top," he said, looking at the boys.

"We'll come up with something," Jumper replied. "How much do we need to raise?"

"A thousand dollars would do it," he said, looking at Jumper.

"That's a lot of money," Jumper mumbled. He thought for a minute. "We could have a bake sale or sell candy or something to help raise the money," he offered.

"Yeah, we'll come up with something," Kelvin agreed.

They left Coach Wright in the building and walked outside.

"Can you come by my house?" Jumper asked as he followed Kelvin and his father to the street. "I'd like you to meet my mother and grandmother," he said to Mr. Francis.

"What do you say, Kelvin?" the father said to his son.

"Let's go," Kelvin replied.

When they got to the brownstone, Jumper introduced Kelvin's dad to his mom.

"Nice to meet you," Carolyn Breeze said as she and Kelvin shook hands.

"You, too," he replied.

"Please come in." Jumper's mother ushered them all into the living room. "Can I get you something to drink?"

"Juice is fine with me," said Mr. Francis. "Whatever you have."

"Kelvin? Jumper?"

"I'll have juice, too, please," Kelvin replied.

"Me, too," said Jumper.

While his mother got the drinks, Jumper showed Mr. Francis around the room.

Mr. Francis stopped by a family photo. "Is that your dad?" he asked.

"Yeah, he had a heart attack and died last winter," Jumper told him.

"Kelvin told me. I was very sorry to hear that you lost your father," Mr. Francis said. He looked closer. "He was a handsome man, Jumper."

"Yeah," Jumper replied. He'd studied this very photo

a million times wondering if he'd look like his father. He quickly put that picture down and picked up another. "This is our old house in Connecticut," he said.

"Now that's living," said Mr. Francis. "I like space between houses and some trees," he added.

"Me, too," agreed Jumper. "But I'm getting used to living in New York now. In Connecticut, my mom had to drive me everywhere. Now I can take the bus and walk to stores — even a video arcade!"

"I guess that's the good part," Mr. Francis said.

Jumper's mom came back into the living room with a tray of glasses.

"I see my son's been giving you our family history," Mrs. Breeze said once they were seated.

"He told me about your husband dying so suddenly," Mr. Francis said. "That must have been hard."

Jumper's mother said nothing for a minute. Then she looked at Jumper and said, "It was . . . still is, but we're doing okay. Our life has changed quite a bit."

"I can tell from the pictures. From the country to the city, from what I see," Mr. Francis said.

"Suburbs, really. The photo looks more country than it was. Our neighbors were pretty close by," Carolyn explained.

Mr. Francis put the photos down and looked up at Jumper's mother. "My son tells me that you teach art," he said.

"Just since my husband died, but I'm loving it. The kids are great," she added.

"First time I ever heard a high school teacher say kids are great," Mr. Francis teased. "You must be some teacher!"

"Mom, is Grandma here?" Jumper interrupted.

"It's swing dance night," his mother answered.

"My grandma's not your usual grandmother," Jumper explained to Mr. Francis. "She owns a Laundromat, holds political meetings in the back, and swing dances twice a week!"

Mr. Francis laughed. "She sounds like fun," he said.

"Oh, she is," Jumper agreed.

"She'll be sorry she missed you, Mr. Francis," Mrs. Breeze said.

"Please call me Francis," he said. "Back home we often go by our last name."

"Okay, Francis, then. Can you stay for dinner? My mother left us a big pan of her delicious macaroni and cheese and greens. I baked a chicken, so there's plenty."

Mr. Francis glanced at the boys and smiled as they nodded. "We'd love to," he said.

Over dinner, they talked about school, student council elections, and basketball.

"Kelvin's dad is going to help us rebuild the gym floor," Jumper told his mom.

"You're a contractor, then?" she asked.

"At home in St. Croix, yes."

"He's going to work for free," Kelvin announced.

"Then you've arrived right on time!" Carolyn said, laughing.

"After the gym floor's laid down, I'd like to take you back with me to St. Croix for a while," Mr. Francis told his son.

"You mean over Christmas like last year?" Kelvin asked.

"I was hoping you'd stay longer this time," he replied.

"I can't. I have to get back to school. Besides, it will be basketball season."

"We have basketball in St. Croix, too," Mr. Francis reminded him.

"I know, but I want to play for Langston Hughes with my friends," Kelvin said.

"That might not be possible," his dad told him.

"What do you mean?" Kelvin asked.

"I want you to get to know the other side of your family, Kelvin. You've got lots of cousins who only get to spend a couple of weeks a year with you and a grandmother who misses you," Mr. Francis said.

"Dad, I can't leave my mother!"

"She'll understand. Your mother's had you for eleven years. I want you to spend some time with me."

"I'm not going!" Kelvin shouted.

"We'll talk about it more later, but you'll do as you're told," Mr. Francis told Kelvin.

Kelvin leaned back in his chair and crossed his arms over his chest. He glared angrily at his father.

"Kelvin talks about St. Croix often," Mrs. Breeze said. "He loves it there. He's even tried to convince my son and me to come down for the Christmas festival, I believe?"

"Yes. You should come down," Mr. Francis said. "We have lots of parties and a big parade similar to a carnival with great costumes and dancing. As an artist, you'd really appreciate the costumes. They're all handmade."

"I hope we can come. If not this year, sometime soon," Mrs. Breeze added.

"Hey, Kelvin, I got a new video game. Want to try it?" Jumper asked Kelvin as they finished eating.

Kelvin shrugged. "Is it any good?"

"It's slammin'! Mom, can Kelvin and I play a few rounds?"

"It's a school night, Jumper," his mother reminded him.

"I know. Please — just ten minutes?" Jumper pleaded.

"All right, but ten minutes — that's all. Friday night's soon enough. Kelvin's welcome to come back then." Mrs. Breeze smiled at Mr. Francis. "I have to set limits or my son wouldn't leave from in front of the television," she said.

Jumper and Kelvin took their dishes to the kitchen, then raced upstairs to Jumper's room.

Kelvin grabbed the controls and started pushing buttons even before the game was loaded.

"You mad?" Jumper asked Kelvin.

"I'm not going. He can't make me!"

"Just play it cool. Talk with your mother. She won't make you go," Jumper suggested.

Kelvin hit play and moved his computer football players down the field. Jumper put his defense into play. As his offensive lineman rammed into Kelvin's quarterback, Kelvin's team lost control of the ball.

"Think he'll still stay and fix the gym floor?" Kelvin asked.

"He'll stay," Jumper said.

"Then I'll talk with my mom," Kelvin replied.

CHAPTER SEVEN

rincipal Young posted election sign-up sheets outside her office. Jumper was the first student to arrive. The page for sixth-grade candidates was blank. He hesitated.

"Is that one name or two?" Nia asked.

Jumper looked around, pressured to make a decision. "Two," he decided, and printed JUMPER BREEZE on the first line.

Smiling, he turned and offered Nia his Sharpie.

"Got my own," she replied, pulling a purple Sharpie out of her backpack.

Jumper stood back while she signed her name on the second line. It was official. He held out his hand to Nia.

"Let the party begin," she said.

"Think anyone else is running for sixth-grade representative?" Jumper asked.

"Not that I've heard. Sign-up's from nine to eleven thirty, so we'll know soon," Nia replied.

"True," Jumper said, then pressed on to his first class.

Jumper was still smiling when he got to English. Their teacher started up a discussion about persuasive writing. He looked back at Nia wondering if she'd say how she planned on persuading kids to vote for her. He had no intention of tipping his hand.

"What's a candidate selling?" Miss Williams asked the class.

"Himself," Dakota called out.

"Ideas," Jumper added.

"She's trying to convince her classmates that she's the right person for the job," Nia said.

They left class with an assignment to write a persuasive essay or poem. That afternoon, Jumper and Kelvin went over to Jumper's house to plot. After a snack, they lay across the beds in Jumper's room listening to CDs and talking.

"Eddie's working on the posters," Jumper told Kelvin.

"That's good, but you've got to get out there big!

Do something different that will get kids' attention," Kelvin said.

"Like what?" Jumper asked.

"I don't know, man. It hasn't come to me yet," Kelvin replied.

"This song's hot," Jumper said. He mouthed the words to his favorite rap tune.

"It's banging," Kelvin said, picking up the chorus.

"I've got it!" Jumper shouted.

"Got what?"

"We'll write a rap song using this beat. You can sing backup. We'll find a couple of other guys, too!" Jumper was on his feet, excited.

"That's it!" Kelvin leapt up. "Juston's the music king. Don't know 'bout Eddie. If he can sing, I'm sure he'd be down with the idea," Kelvin added. "Play that song again and let's start writing some words."

The boys worked on the song, then practiced it until they had it memorized. They e-mailed Juston and Eddie the words and told them to be ready to perform!

The next day as the sixth graders filed into the cafeteria, they were surprised by music blasting through a boom box. Jumper waited until a crowd had gathered around, then he turned the music down some and sang his song:

> *My name is Elijah*
> *Friends call me Jumper*
> *I want to get to know ya*
> *So today I'm a rapper*
> *Don't be fooled basketball's my game*
> *Don't be lame*
> *Don't be shy*
> *Meet me on the courts*
> *And see me jump high*
> *But I want to represent*
> *Not just on the court*
> *So vote me in and see how I support ya . . .*

Kelvin, Juston, and Eddie backed Jumper up. They started the chorus, telling the other students to join in: *Jump up for Jumper, Jump UP!*

Kids danced and clapped as Jumper repeated his rap several times. The performance only lasted a few minutes, but Jumper was now firmly launched as a candidate for student council.

Nia watched from across the cafeteria, annoyed that she hadn't thought of something better than balloons, posters, and silly flyers! She walked around the cafeteria telling groups of students that she was also running for sixth-grade representative only to be greeted by praise for Jumper.

"That was the best!" they raved.

"He's fun!"

"Plus he can sing!"

Nia walked up to a group of girls and introduced herself. "Hi, I'm Nia," she said. "I'm running for student council. I want to be your sixth-grade representative."

"Oh. Hi, I'm Jamilla. These are my friends Jazz and Brooklyn," one girl said.

"Nice to meet you," Nia replied, handing each girl one of her flyers.

"Girls can be basketball players, too!" Jamilla read aloud. "Like we didn't know that."

"We do, but still, it took a few girls standing up to get a girls' basketball team at Langston," Nia reminded Jamilla.

"Girl power!" Jamilla shouted. "I'm with you."

"Nia, we also need help with the music program. Why don't you make that happen, too?" Jazz asked.

"Just stick with me and I will!" Nia promised. "I didn't see you at basketball practice. Do you play?"

"Only the flute," Jazz replied.

"Gotcha," Nia replied.

"I used to play basketball," Brooklyn began. "I'd like to join the team."

"I don't know. Since *these* started growing," Jazz said, giggling and pointing to her chest, "I haven't played sports as much."

The girls laughed with her.

"I'm going to play all the way through college," Nia stated. "Might even go for the pros."

"You're that good?"

"You know it," Nia answered. "You should come by and see us play. We could use some more girls on the team."

"I'm confused. If there's no gym, how can there be a basketball program?" Brooklyn asked.

"The girls practice in the gym at the YMCA and the boys practice in the yard. Mr. Wright is getting the gym floor fixed. We need to help raise money. We're having our second practice tomorrow. Why don't you come out?" Nia asked the girls. "And if I'm elected, I'll look into that music program," she added.

The girls looked at each other. "That'll work," Jazz said.

Nia continued to make her rounds. Each time she walked up to a group, they had Jumper's name on their lips. The students accepted her flyers, but it was clear that their focus was all about Jumper.

Nia walked out of the cafeteria frustrated. She'd have to come up with something exciting quick!

"Hey, sis, what's up?" Marcus asked when he bumped into her.

"I messed up," Nia told her brother.

"How?" Marcus asked.

"I should have come up with a better way to announce my candidacy. Something fun like Jumper did," she said.

"I heard," he said.

"Everyone who comes through here tells me what fun they had or how silly Jumper is. It's . . . it's frustrating!" she said. "I've got to turn things around or kiss the election good-bye!" she told him.

"What are you gonna do?" Marcus asked.

"I haven't the slightest idea," Nia replied. "What's up with you?"

"Got basketball practice this afternoon. It makes no

sense to me when we don't have a gym," Marcus complained.

"Don't worry. Mr. Wright will take care of that," Nia said.

"How'd your practice go?" Marcus asked.

"Oh, we've got a pretty good team. Miss King is a great coach. The girls are all about basketball and a couple of new recruits just joined," she replied.

"Where are you playing?"

"The gym at the Y for now," Nia said.

"That's better than the yard with its uneven cement," Marcus reminded her.

"How's your team?" Nia asked her brother.

"We've got some good players. Your friend Jumper's one of the best players out there. Surprised me after how he bombed out in baseball," Marcus said.

"Hey!" Nia cried.

"What?"

"I just got a great idea!" Nia replied.

"What's that?" Marcus asked.

"How 'bout if I convince the girls to challenge the boys in a basketball game! We could make it a fundraiser for the gym. Bet we could raise that money needed to finish the floor!" Nia suggested.

"Are you crazy?" Marcus said. "I thought you wanted to look good. The boys will smash the girls!"

"I don't think so!" Nia shot back.

"Go ahead. Make it happen but don't come crying to me when we win!" Marcus said.

"You'll be the one bawling and embarrassed when we outplay you!" Nia warned. "So get in shape, brother. I'm taking you on!"

"Get ready to be disgraced," Marcus shot back.

Both coaches bought into Nia's challenge. The big game was set for Friday night. With a date set, the teams scheduled extra practice sessions. Nia sent out flyers announcing the challenge and fund-raising goal. It was a major piece of her campaign.

Jumper's campaign was also in full swing. Eddie had the Web site up and running by the second day of the campaign. Jumper's home page featured him making a layup shot. One of the links took you to Jumper singing his rap song, which announced his campaign. Jumper set aside an hour a day to write a blog. The first day Jumper's site was up, it got fifty hits!

It was Juston who came up with the idea for pencils. He complained that there were never enough pencils in the classrooms. Students were always asking to borrow one. Eddie printed out labels from his computer and the boys taped them to the pencils.

The second day of the campaign, Jumper and Kelvin stood near the lockers and handed out pencils with his slogan taped across them. *Jump up for Jumper* was everywhere!

The pencils were a big hit!

"Free? Cool!" said one kid.

"Jump up for Jumper." A girl read the slogan out loud. "Cute," she said.

"Can I have two?" one boy wanted to know.

Jumper smiled and greeted each student.

"Hi, my name's Brittany. You're a really good singer," a girl said.

"Hey, can you dance, too?" her friend asked.

Jumper blushed. "Not very well," he replied.

"Bet you'd be good in one of those video game dance tournaments," Brittany continued. "We're having one at the arcade on Saturday afternoon. Come on by."

Jumper looked at Kelvin and shrugged. "Thanks for letting us know," he said.

The girls walked on.

"Not a bad idea," Kelvin said.

"What, dancing in the tournament?" Jumper asked.

"Yeah, but coming up with a character and performing as it. Let's check it out after school. Find out the music and plan on entering. A lot of kids from school will be there," Kelvin suggested.

"You mean dressing up like Astro or something?" Jumper asked, thinking of the dance tournaments he'd seen in the past. The best dancers were always in costume.

"I'm game if you are. It'll be fun," Kelvin urged.

"Okay. I'll mention it to Nia and Dakota. Maybe they'll want to enter, too," Jumper said.

The bell rang for class.

"Thanks for your help, campaign manager," Jumper said, gathering up his backpack. He and Kelvin knocked knuckles and headed to separate classes.

Jumper was on the steps at the front of the school at three fifteen when Kelvin and Juston found him.

"Come on, Jumper, we've got to find out what music they're using for the tournament," Juston said.

"Yeah, and learn dance steps in five days," Jumper added. "That's impossible! I'm not making a fool of myself."

"You won't," Juston told him.

"Jumper's right," Kelvin said, dropping down on one of the steps. "It sounded like a good idea, but we don't have the time to get it together. Besides, I have to meet my father at four thirty," he groaned.

Jumper sat down beside Kelvin.

"Did you get things worked out?" Jumper asked.

"You mean about my living in St. Croix for a while?"

Jumper nodded.

"My parents talked and agreed that it was up to me," Kelvin replied.

"So are you going or not?" Jumper asked.

"I told my dad I'd let him know before he leaves," Kelvin said.

Jumper checked his watch. "If we hurry, you can go with us to the arcade and still make it home in time to meet your dad," Jumper suggested.

"Then you really think we should enter?" asked Kelvin.

"You said I had to have some fun in my campaign!" Jumper replied.

"Let's go, then," Juston said.

"Are the girls coming?" Kelvin asked as they headed to the arcade.

Nia and Dakota were already at the arcade when the boys arrived. They were studying the music list. "Hey, guys," Nia said, looking up.

"Hi, Nia. How's it going?"

"Not bad. I ran into Principal Young. She got a few businesses to sponsor the basketball game. If we sell raffle tickets and admission, we should raise a lot of money."

"Enough for the gym floor?" Jumper asked.

"The principal thinks we'll raise enough for the floor, new basketball hoops, and uniforms for the boys and girls!" Nia reported.

"That's amazing!" Dakota beamed.

"Works for me," Jumper said.

"Me, too," Kelvin agreed.

"Speaking of outfits: Are you wearing a costume to the dance tournament?" Nia asked.

"I think so," Jumper replied.

"That'll be crazy! Who are you gonna be?" Nia asked.

"Don't know yet," Jumper said.

"Come on, Nia. I've got to get home," Dakota said.

As Nia turned to leave, she remembered her name tags. While the boys were distracted with the music list,

Nia slapped them on their backpacks. She winked at Dakota as they made a quick exit.

Before they left, Jumper and Juston threw the backpacks over their shoulders completely unaware of the tags that read: HI, I'M NIA; VOTE FOR MEA!

CHAPTER EIGHT

With seven days to campaign hard, Jumper and Nia cranked up their efforts.

"Let's go over the schedule," Kelvin suggested. "We've got a little over a week. We'll keep working the hallways at school. The pencils are popular so we'll keep handing them out. We've got the game Friday night. Then we can focus on the dance tournament. You know, use the weekend to practice our dance routines. Then next Saturday is the dance tournament, which will give us Sunday for the final campaign push. Monday's election day so we need to work on your speech. By Monday afternoon, you'll be our representative!"

"That's a lot," Jumper said.

"Sure is, but then things will settle back down," Kelvin reminded him.

"I wonder what Nia's up to now?" Juston asked.

"Don't know, but how long did you walk around with her campaign tag on your backpack?" Jumper asked.

"I found it when I got home," Juston said.

"'Hi, I'm Nia; vote for mea!' How corny." Kelvin cracked up.

"Yeah, well, I walked around with it plastered to my backpack and didn't even notice it!" Jumper said.

"Guess she got one over on you," Kelvin said. "But if her speech is as lame as her slogan, you'll sail through this election."

"Hope mine isn't lame, too," Jumper replied.

"Our outline rocked!"

"Let's hope the speech will, too," Jumper said.

"You straight on the schedule?" Kelvin asked.

"Yes, but you sound like my homeroom teacher," Jumper said.

"It's my job," Kelvin reminded him.

"Got it," Jumper replied.

❈ ❈ ❈

The same day, Dakota and Sabrina drilled Nia.

"How's your speech coming?" Dakota asked in the locker room before basketball practice.

"It's been done," Nia boasted.

"Did you memorize it?" Sabrina asked.

Nia frowned at her friend. "That's not necessary," she replied.

"Did you read it out loud to anyone?" Dakota asked.

"No," Nia said defensively.

"I want to hear it," Sabrina insisted.

"Why?"

"Because you need to rehearse for a speech just like you do for a basketball game. You could lose just because you give a lame speech," Dakota reminded her.

"I know that!" Nia replied.

"Good, then after the game you can give the speech to me or Sabrina," Dakota said.

Nia groaned. "Can't. I've got plans for Saturday," she reminded her friends.

"Sunday, then," Dakota decided. "We can meet at my house and go over it."

"I was planning on sleeping all day," Nia teased.

"You can sleep after the elections," Dakota said.

"Gotcha."

"Come on . . . this is our last practice. You've got to work on your jump shot so you'll look good tomorrow night!" Dakota said.

Game night, the gym at the YMCA was packed. The boys were already on the courts when the girls showed up. They tossed the ball using quick, hard chest passes. Every time one of the boys lifted into the air and took a jump shot, the boys in the stands went wild.

Nia peeked from behind the bleachers and spied on the opposition. Her teammates lined up behind her.

"They look pretty good," Sabrina whispered.

"Wow," Callie said as Jumper landed an incredible jump shot.

"Okay, they're pretty, but do they look like a team?" Nia asked. The boys were wearing the jerseys of their favorite pro basketball players. Each jersey was a different color and so were the boys' shorts. Nia looked back at her teammates. They all wore white T-shirts with their name and number printed on the back. They looked together . . . like a team. Nia smiled. "We can win! Let's go!"

The girls huddled for a group hug. "Play ball!" they

shouted, and sprinted through the bleachers and onto the court to a standing ovation.

Jumper and Kelvin stopped throwing jump shots and turned to look at the girls.

"Man, they look . . ." Kelvin hesitated.

"Serious," Jumper offered.

"I heard they were gonna wear costumes," Kelvin said.

Jumper held back a laugh. "So you thought they'd wear skirts and high-heeled sneakers, right?"

"Word! Instead they look . . ." Kelvin was stumped again.

"They look better than us, man. You see those matching mesh shorts, big white T-shirts . . . new sneakers! Come on, let's go shake their hands," Jumper urged. He called his teammates and motioned toward the girls.

"What you want, man?" Marcus asked.

"Think we should greet our opposing team," Jumper suggested.

"For what?" Marcus asked.

"Good sportsmanship," Kelvin said.

Marcus turned away, whispering under his breath.

"You go on over there if you want. I'm going back to shoot some baskets."

"Come on, Marcus," Jumper insisted.

"Yeah. Come on, Marcus," the other boys chimed in.

Marcus hesitated. "All right," he said.

The boys assembled in the middle of the court. They turned to walk toward the girls, but the girls were already well on their way toward the boys.

"Embarrassing," Jumper whispered to Kelvin as they stood still. Jumper stepped forward and extended his hand. "Hey, Nia," he said.

"Hey. We just wanted to wish you the best." Nia spoke for her team.

"Back at you," Jumper replied.

The girls ran up and down the court to warm up. Several balls were in constant motion as each girl practiced shooting. The boys watched. Jumper saw that the girls' accuracy matched the boys'.

"Could be a tough game," he said to Kelvin.

A whistle blew. Coach Wright and Miss King, the girls' coach, announced the lineup and the referee set up the jump shot. Jumper and Callie faced off in the circle along the mid-court line.

"Play ball!" the referee yelled, and threw the basket-ball straight up into the air. Jumper lifted his long, lean body, tipped the ball away from Callie, and sent it straight into Marcus's hands.

Sabrina flew down the court as Marcus drove to the basket. Reaching Marcus, she got into defensive position, stayed low, shuffled her feet from side to side, and waved her hands.

Blocked from his shot, Marcus bounce-passed the ball to Kelvin, who cut to the basket and made an easy layup. Score!

Brooklyn whipped around Kelvin, jumped up, and grabbed the ball as it passed through the hoop.

"Go!" Coach King yelled from the sidelines.

Nia took off, dribbling hard and fast, straight down the center. She was flanked by Callie and Dakota. Jumper was hot on their tail. He overtook Callie just as Nico gained on Nia.

"Dakota, ball!" Nia yelled, and chest-passed the basketball to Dakota.

Dakota caught the pass and shot just as Marcus pounced in front of her. The ball hit the backboard and slipped into the basket to score two points.

"Way to go!" Nia shouted.

Jumper snatched the rebound and took off.

"I got ball," Callie signaled to her teammates as she sprinted upcourt next to Jumper.

Callie blocked Jumper's chest pass to Kelvin and caught the ball. She pivoted, spotted an open player, and bounce-passed to Brooklyn.

Brooklyn cut right, losing Kelvin, and drove on toward the hoop. She turned her head to check her wings and lost her concentration for a second. Kelvin was right there to take advantage of the distraction. He grabbed the ball out of Brooklyn's hands, pivoted, and quickly passed to Marcus.

Marcus drove to the basket while Sabrina desperately tried to block him. Marcus switched hands, spun around, and lifted into the air before Sabrina could get back into defensive position. The ball hit the rim, circled it a couple of times, and dropped into the basket!

The boys whooped. "Nice shot!" Jumper shouted from across the court. The ball was still in play.

Callie was near the basket. She jumped up and grabbed the rebound.

Marcus slapped the ball out of her hands as she landed, pivoted so that his back was to Callie, then went up for another jump shot. *Swish!*

"Two!" the referee screamed.

The game moved fast, with the girls keeping pace with the boys in what looked to be an evenly matched game. They battled until the referee signaled the end of the first quarter. The score was boys 18, girls 16.

The starters, joined by the other girls on the bench, gathered with Coach King. "Good job. I'm sending in Jamilla for Callie. Lilli, you take over for Dakota. Stay on your man! Don't let up! You've got the boys in speed and smarts," Coach King instructed. "Some uniforms on those boys, huh, girls," she teased. "But you look good. Like a team!"

Across the court, the boys huddled with Coach Wright. Jumper was irritated that he'd yet to score a jump shot while Marcus had already scored ten points!

"He's hogging the ball," Jumper whispered to Kelvin.

No names were needed. Kelvin understood. "Word," he replied. "At least keeping it from you. Get aggressive," Kelvin replied.

"Gotcha!" Jumper shot back. Kelvin was right: This was no time to be nice.

"Stay with me. Your time is now!" Kelvin told Jumper.

"Jumper. Kelvin," Coach Wright called them out. "This is not the time for a private conversation," he reminded them. "These girls are on it today. You all need to pump it up a notch! Play hard! Play fair! Play as a team!"

The boys whooped and slapped five as they broke from their circle and rejoined the girls on the court. The crowd cheered as the teams returned to play.

"Let's go girls! Let's go girls!" fans yelled from the stands. Big signs went up across the bleachers reading: GIRL POWER! VOTE FOR NIA! NIA FOR STUDENT COUNCIL!

On the courts, Jumper simmered. Why hadn't he thought to make signs?

"Ball!" Kelvin yelled, and cut to Jumper.

Jumper ran toward Kelvin. They met shoulder-to-shoulder, with Kelvin between Jumper and Jamilla. Kelvin passed the ball off to Jumper and quickly cut toward the basket.

Jumper dribbled, switching hands as he dodged past Jamilla. He sent a bounce pass to Kelvin, who went in for a layup.

"Two!" the referee yelled. He blew the whistle, retrieved the ball, and tossed it to Jamilla for her to throw back into play.

Jamilla's toss successfully reached Brooklyn. She took two dribbles, then passed to Lilli, who continued toward their basket. Lilli's pass to Sabrina was intercepted by Juston, who pivoted and dribbled downcourt. Once past the mid-court line, Juston passed to Francisco, who immediately shot it to Eddie, who'd come up from the corner. Eddie leapt into the air, shooting over the top of his defenders. The ball sank into the basket without touching the rim. *Swish!*

Brooklyn snatched the rebound and took off down the floor. Nia and Lilli flanked her. When Brooklyn reached half-court, Nia and Lilli switched places. Nico and Juston scrambled to keep up with them. Brooklyn used the opportunity to chest pass to Nia. The ball hit the backboard on the edge, wobbled, then dropped into the basket. Nia's cheering squad in the stands jumped to their feet, shouting her name and waving her signs.

The girls were hot!

At halftime the score was 26 to 28. The girls screamed and waved to their fans as they left the court. Inside the locker room, they regrouped with their coach.

On the opposite side of the court, the boys raged at one another.

"Told you this wasn't gonna be no piece of cake!" Juston said.

"They're just up by two. We'll get it back and more next quarter," Marcus replied. He squirted a chilled sports drink down his throat.

"Don't be so sure of yourself!" Jumper shot back.

Coach Wright walked into the locker room and stopped the bickering. "Keep this up and you'll give the game to the girls," he reminded them. They talked strategy for the second half.

"Now I have some good news: Principal Young just told me and Coach King that the money from tonight's game put us over the top," said Coach Wright. "Boys, we have a gym floor!"

The boys clapped, stomped, and whistled.

"Way to go, Coach!" they cheered.

"Hey. It was a team effort! Now let's go out there and play what?" Coach yelled.

"Play hard!" they yelled back.

"And?"

"Play fair!" the boys called out.

"And?"

"Play as a team!"

CHAPTER NINE

The referees blew their whistles. Game time!

Marcus sprinted downcourt with Jumper and Kelvin as his wingmen. They moved with such force that they left their guards trailing. When Marcus entered the end zone, he lifted into the air and took the shot. *Swish!*

"Two!"

Sabrina grabbed the rebound, passed to Dakota, who passed it on to Callie, who sent it flying back to Dakota. While Dakota cut to the basket, Sabrina screened Nia from Nico. Dakota took the shot.

"Two!" the referee yelled.

The time sped by with the girls leading by two. With

two minutes remaining, the score was girls 46, boys 44. Coach Wright signaled for a time-out. The referee called it.

The boys and girls gathered around their coaches to strategize. At the whistle, they ran back onto the court to finish the game. It was the boys' ball. Nico stood behind the defensive end line. Keeping her distance, Nia waved her hands and danced from side to side, trying to block Nico's pass.

Nico dodged her hand with a successful overhead pass to Jumper.

Jumper dribbled the ball slowly, ignoring Callie's blocking efforts. At mid-court, he sprinted toward the basket while Callie kept in step.

Juston was to Jumper's left. Dakota guarded him closely. Kelvin was in the right corner, but Brooklyn was on him like gnats to ankles on a hot summer evening. Kelvin dodged and darted without losing his shadow. Jumper dribbled on, seeing that Sabrina had Marcus tied up.

The seconds ticked away.

The crowd was on their feet, shouting for their teams.

Jumper switched hands as he bounced the ball

between his legs. He cut hard. Right then left. Callie stayed right with him, using her arms and body as a shield. With no other option, Jumper lifted for a shot.

Callie jumped into the air with him, equally determined to block the shot. She lifted her hands, reached for the ball, and grabbed Jumper's right arm by mistake.

The referee whistled and yelled: "Hand contact! Foul on number twenty. Two shots for Jumper!"

The crowd hushed.

Fifteen seconds remained!

Jumper warmed up at the free-throw line. Marcus, Kelvin, Juston, and Nico lined up on one side; Nia, Sabrina, Dakota, Callie, and Brooklyn stood across from them.

"You got it!" Kelvin called to him.

"Make it two!" Juston added.

Jumper nodded toward his teammates. He bounced the ball several times and got into position. He was so nervous. Then he bent his knees, spread his feet, squared his body with the basket, and lifted the ball over his head.

Release!

All eyes followed the ball's flight. It dipped slightly, grazing the inside of the basket.

Jumper sucked in air; his heart pounded.

The ball teetered on the edge for what seemed like forever. *Go in!* he commanded silently.

Go in!

The ball dipped through the hoop.

Jumper whirled around and planted a high five on Kelvin's open hand. The boys' team now trailed the girls by only one point.

Annoyed, Nia leaned over and whispered into Callie's ear.

Marcus eased closer to the basket, anticipating a rush for the rebound.

Callie eyed Marcus cautiously. She stepped closer to the basket and smiled sweetly at Marcus.

Jumper repositioned his body, bent down, lifted his arms, and propelled the basketball with his fingertips.

Swish! Tied! 46 to 46!

Callie took the basketball and stood behind the line. She held the ball tight against her chest. Suddenly, Nia darted in front of her and Callie shot her the ball.

With no one guarding her, Nia sped past Nico and drove downcourt. The floor was wide open. Sabrina sprinted to Nia's right. Marcus lifted his right arm, prepared to block Nia's pass.

Brooklyn held back with Kelvin, prepared to defend should the girls lose control of the ball. Jumper stayed on Callie as she made her way downcourt behind Nia.

Nia glanced right, then left. She lifted into the air and released the ball as the clock ticked down. Two seconds remained.

The ball sailed through the air, hit the rim, and spun around. On its second rotation, the clock ticked down to one second. When Nia's feet hit the floor, she froze. Had she made the right decision? Or did her bold move cost the girls the game? Nia stared at the basket, holding her breath as the ball circled the rim twice. On the second swirl, the ball tipped and sank into the basket, just as the buzzer sounded.

48 to 46. Girls!

Jumper froze. They'd been beaten by a bunch of sixth-grade girls! Kids poured out of the bleachers, streamed onto the court, and surrounded the girls. A couple of them paraded around, holding Nia up.

Nia laughed and pumped her arms into the air.

"I'm mad," Kelvin said as he moved in next to Jumper.

"Me, too. We should have won," Jumper said.

Kelvin looked over at Marcus. "Big shot hogged the ball," Kelvin grumbled.

Jumper glanced over at Marcus without commenting. He and the rest of the boys' team watched in stunned silence.

Coach King broke into the center of the celebration and moved her girls through the crowd.

"Manners!" she shouted, and pointed toward the boys' team.

"Let's go, girls!" Nia shouted, and led the way.

"Nice game," Jumper whispered to Nia when they reached for each other's hand.

"You, too," she replied.

As soon as the hand-shaking was done, the teams split to their respective locker rooms.

Jumper and Kelvin crossed the court to the locker room without speaking. Nia had saved the game! If there'd been an MVP vote, she would have won. The boys would be laughed out of school. His campaign was dead! If only he'd gotten the ball more!

Inside the locker room, Coach Wright attempted to cheer up his gloomy team. "Okay, so we've got some work to do," Coach Wright told them. "But if you want to win, you'll have to start working as a team."

Jumper looked around, his arms resting on his knees. Marcus was staring at the floor, his hands clenched. Why did it always come down to him and Marcus? Jumper wondered. While they played this on-and-off game, their team lost.

Jumper stood up and joined his teammates in the circle. He folded his hands in with the others, and lifted them as they shouted: "Teamwork!"

The boys emptied their lockers and headed out.

"By now Nia will have called half of the school," Nico said on the way out.

"Yeah, she's got a mouth on her. She'll have the whole school thinking that the girls carried the game all the way through," Kelvin added.

"Good news about the gym, though," Jumper offered.

"Nice jump shot," Eddie called over to him.

"Too bad you didn't get the ball more," Juston said. He shot an angry look toward Marcus. "If you had, you would have sunk that bad boy in a few more times."

"No telling," Jumper said. It was just too easy to

blame it all on Marcus; it wasn't right, he decided. "We played a good game. All of us," he reminded Juston. There was always a "what if" when it came to a loss. Always someone blaming someone else, as if the fault rested with one person.

Kelvin came up beside Jumper. "We're a team, remember?"

"Gotcha," Juston said, tossing his basketball back into his locker and slamming the door shut. He slapped Jumper and Kelvin a high five. "See ya," he said, and walked out of the locker room.

Jumper looked around. The room was empty except for Kelvin and Marcus. Jumper watched as Marcus pulled his jeans over his basketball trunks and slowly looked up.

"Got something to say to me?" Marcus asked.

"Not really," Jumper replied. He zipped his backpack closed.

Marcus walked over to Jumper and Kelvin. "This team stinks!"

"We had it and you messed up!" Kelvin retorted.

"Yeah, right. Where were you? No one was open and ready for a pass," he fought back.

"Did you look?" Kelvin asked, stepping closer to Marcus.

Jumper stepped between them. "We've got some work to do, that's all. We'll come back. Stronger. Better."

"That's if Marcus doesn't hog the ball," Kelvin replied.

The boys looked toward Marcus. It was up to him.

Marcus shoved his hands in his pockets and shuffled his feet. Slowly, he lifted his head and faced Jumper and Kelvin. "No need to. It's a good team. I can see that you're a lot better at basketball then baseball," he said to Jumper.

It wasn't exactly a compliment, but Jumper got the point. It was the best Marcus could do. "Good, then next time pass me the ball," he said.

"Gotcha," Marcus replied.

"I'm outta here, man. My dad's waiting," Kelvin said.

"Let's go," Jumper said, looking at Marcus.

Marcus picked up his backpack and lifted it to one shoulder. "Let's move," he said, cracking his first smile of the evening.

As they plowed through the locker room door, Jumper spotted his grandmother headed their way.

"Hey, Grams," Jumper called to her. "You remember Marcus from baseball camp," he said as the boys approached. Jumper looked for his mother and spotted her talking with Kelvin's dad and Coach Wright.

Jumper waved. His mom smiled and waved back. He watched as she broke away and headed toward him.

"Oh, yes," Miss BB replied. "Glad to finally put a face with the name. I'm Jumper's grandmother. You can call me Miss BB," she offered.

Marcus took Jumper's grandmother's hand. "Nice to meet you, Miss BB," he said politely.

"Hey, Miss BB," Kelvin broke in. "What'd you think of the game?"

Jumper groaned.

She chuckled. "Guess you boys will suffer for a bit, but you played well, so don't carry on too long, you hear?"

"I got you," Kelvin replied.

"The girls will keep it alive," Jumper reminded them.

"Only if you let them. Blow it off. It's a loss, not the end of the world. Figure out how you can improve and move on. The girls will get the message. Now, if you agonize, the story will have long legs."

"Your grandmother's got a point," Jumper's mom chimed in. "Besides, both teams played well. And this fund-raiser was good news for Langston Hughes. After all, when it comes to fixing the gym, you're on the same side," she told the boys.

"Speaking of moving on, you boys joining us for Saturday-night dinner and Scrabble?" Miss BB asked.

Marcus looked at her with questioning eyes.

"It's a tradition we started when Jumper and his mom moved in," she explained. "Kelvin usually comes. You're welcome, too," Miss BB added.

"Can't come this week, Miss BB. I have to go visit my father's family," Kelvin replied.

"Well, that's important. But I'll miss beating you at Scrabble," she said, laughing. "Marcus, you up for the challenge?"

"Uh . . ." he muttered, not sure what to say.

"He's busy, Grandma," Jumper spoke for Marcus. He didn't want Marcus coming to his house, especially since Kelvin wouldn't be there.

"Is that true?" Mrs. Breeze asked Marcus.

"Uh . . ." Marcus said.

"Don't let my mother intimidate you," Mrs. Breeze said, laughing. "It's a fun night, right, boys?"

"Usually," Jumper agreed, thinking that could change if Marcus showed up.

Kelvin's dad joined them. "Nice game, boys," he said.

"Coulda done better," Kelvin replied.

"That's true. And you will," Mr. Francis said.

"Dad, this is Jumper's grandmother, Miss BB," Kelvin said.

"You're from St. Croix, Jumper tells me," Miss BB said in greeting. "I was on one of those cruises. We stopped in St. Croix. In Fredriksted, I believe?"

"Yes. That's the town where ships dock. I live there."

"Pretty place," Miss BB said.

"If you like green hills and blue water," Mr. Francis joked.

"Getting back to tomorrow night," said Miss BB. "Kelvin tells us that you can't join us for dinner. Scrabble's more fun when played with a group."

"We're going to my brother's for dinner," Mr. Francis replied.

"Well, then keep next Saturday open. I need Kelvin on my Scrabble team. He's a pretty good speller, you know?" Miss BB said.

Mr. Francis laughed. "We'll be there."

Jumper spotted Nia and called her over.

"Well, here's the star of the game. MVP, right?" Kelvin's dad asked.

"Thanks, Mr. Francis," Nia said, beaming.

"Yes, that was quite a play," Jumper's mom agreed.

"Thank you, Mrs. Breeze," Nia said. She eyed the boys.

Miss BB thumped Jumper on his shoulder. He glared at Nia. "I already told her nice game," he said. But his annoyance was quickly replaced with an idea. If Nia came to dinner on Saturday, too, he wouldn't have to spend time alone with Marcus. "Hey, Nia, why don't you come to dinner at my house tomorrow with Marcus?" Jumper suggested.

"*What?*" Nia asked. Jumper was inviting Marcus over to his house for dinner? That didn't add up. "Are you having a party or something?"

"No," said Jumper, staring directly — and he hoped pointedly — at Nia. "It's just dinner and Scrabble with my mother and grandmother," he explained.

Nia looked up at her brother, but couldn't read him. She glanced back at Jumper. He met her gaze and smiled, wanting her to understand that she should say yes. Nia returned Jumper's smile. "I'd love to come!" she said.

Yes! Now Jumper wouldn't be stuck alone with Marcus.

"Good. You can be on my team for Scrabble, so bring your brains along," Miss BB told Nia. "You can spell, can't you?" she asked.

"Oh, don't worry, Miss BB, I'm a good speller," Nia replied, winking.

Jumper smiled. *We'll see about that,* he thought. He wasn't about to lose to Nia two nights in a row!

"We better get going. Your mother left and promised she'd have dessert and hot chocolate waiting for us at home," Mr. Francis said to his son.

"Did you cook?" Jumper asked his mom.

"Hungry, huh?"

"Starving," he replied.

"We've got to go, too," Marcus said, shoving his sister.

"We'll see you tomorrow around six, then," Mrs. Breeze told them as she left with her son and mother in tow. Once they were outside, she turned to Jumper. "You didn't seem too happy that Marcus and Nia are coming for dinner."

"They're the last two people I want over," he grumbled.

"Then why'd you invite Nia?" Miss BB asked.

"'Cause you'd invited Marcus. At least I won't have to face him alone," Jumper replied.

"It's time you boys became friends," Miss BB insisted.

"Why?"

"Because you're on the same team and you might have won tonight if you hadn't been battling so," Jumper's grandmother replied.

"Mom, that's enough!" said Mrs. Breeze.

"Well, it's true," continued Miss BB. "Those two have been at war since this summer. It makes no sense," she said. "Marcus is not a bad boy, far as I can tell."

"He's just being nice around you, that's all," Jumper threw in.

"From what you've said, Marcus and Nia have problems at home. That may be why Marcus acts up with you. He probably thinks you have no problems. Am I right?" Jumper's mom asked.

"Yeah, but he's wrong."

"Well, then maybe you two have more in common than you think. Give him a chance," Mrs. Breeze suggested.

Jumper was quiet as the three of them walked home.

He didn't respond to his mother, but her voice stayed in his head. He had to admit that Marcus's attitude was better. When Jumper had invited him to join the boys' basketball team, he'd agreed. True, Marcus hogged the ball, but it was their first time playing as a team. He'd even thrown a backhanded compliment Jumper's way. Not to mention, Marcus had agreed to come to his house for dinner. So, maybe his mom had a point. For the sake of the basketball team, he was willing to cut Marcus some slack. But friends? That was a whole different ball game.

CHAPTER TEN

"Boy, what's wrong with you?" Miss BB asked when Jumper came down to the kitchen for the tenth time. She was busy fixing dinner. "If you've got nothing better to do, you could help me fix these greens. Here," she said, handing her grandson a leafy bunch of collards. "Wash them good."

He stood in the middle of the room holding the greens helplessly.

"Here," Miss BB offered, moving over to give her grandson room to work.

Jumper turned on the water and held the greens under the faucet mindlessly.

"Now you know how to clean greens. Come on, fill

up the sink and let them soak while you scrub," Miss BB prodded.

"Can you be friends with someone you don't like?" Jumper asked as he held the greens under the water with his right hand and controlled the faucet with his left.

Miss BB stopped cutting up the greens. Still holding the knife in her hand, she turned to face Jumper. "What?"

"Can you be friends with someone you don't like?" he repeated.

"Are you talking about Marcus?"

"Of course."

"Well, my answer is, you have to get to know someone before you decide not to like them. True, you and Marcus got off wrong, but you're making progress. Him coming over here tonight's huge." She chuckled. "I'm proud of both of you."

"He hasn't come yet," Jumper said.

"Neither has six o'clock. He'll come. Trust me. The boy needs friends and family just as much as you do."

"You know he got kicked out of Catholic school," Jumper reminded his grandmother.

"So you said. I wonder why?"

"Me, too. He's not saying."

"It's his business," Miss BB said.

"I know, but I still want to know," Jumper insisted.

"Why's that?"

"Not sure," Jumper admitted.

"How much does Marcus know about your life?" Miss BB asked.

Jumper shrugged. "Not much."

"Why's that?" his grandmother asked.

"I haven't told him, that's why," Jumper replied.

"My point exactly. Personal information comes with trust. Or should, at least. Neither of you should be sharing too much 'til you establish a friendship. In that process, you'll share. See how it goes tonight," Miss BB suggested.

"Okay," said Jumper.

"Let's talk about the student council elections. It's soon, right?"

"Yeah. We have a little over a week. Elections are the first," Jumper replied.

"How are you feeling about it?"

Jumper stuffed the green leaves into the sink and let them float in the water. He walked over to the counter and climbed onto a stool. The elections were *really* worrying him. He didn't want to lose.

Jumper crossed his arms and lay his head in his hands. "I'm worried," he said.

Miss BB walked over to the counter and stood facing her grandson. "Okay, tell me about it," she said, leaning her hips against the counter.

"Nia was popular even before the basketball game. Now that the girls won, she'll surely win the election," he said.

"You mean because she made that bold winning basket?" Miss BB asked.

Jumper nodded.

"But you did your part. You made both free-throw shots."

"I know, but no one will remember that. They'll just remember Nia grabbing the ball and racing down the court in the final seconds. Plus, she made her jump shot. And she's short!"

"So, she's got talent. So do you," Miss BB responded.

"Yeah, but I'm a tall boy. Everyone expects me to make my shots. I mean, I was surprised! I was certain that Nia would miss that basket."

"But she didn't. That being said, the next week is critical," said Miss BB. "You'll need a game plan for each day. You know how the politicians do it. The closer it gets to election day, the heavier they are with their radio and television ads. Scale that down, of course, but the result is the same. You've got to make sure every sixth grader knows your name."

"I know. We've got a lot going on. We have a week to campaign around school, then the video dance tournament at the arcade, not to mention my speech," he said.

"That is a lot!" Miss BB said. "What's that video dance one about?"

"They're popular at arcades. It's a game. There's a dance pad with arrows. You stand facing the video screen. It also has arrows that light up to the beat of the music. They tell you where to step. It's quick. Like a dance. Kids get fancy with their steps and throw in some flips and things," Jumper explained. "You can dress up as one of the characters. And a judge keeps score."

"Man, that's complicated. Are you any good at that?" Miss BB asked.

"I used to play when I lived in Connecticut. I'm pretty good, but Kelvin says that even if I mess up that's okay. He wants kids to see me having fun."

"I see. You've got a lot going on."

"Tell me about it. I've got to go call Kelvin," he said, hopping off the stool. He turned to leave, and then remembered the greens. "Uh, Grandma . . ."

She smiled. "Go ahead, boy. I'll finish washing the greens."

Jumper waved as he rushed off to call Kelvin.

After talking with Kelvin, Jumper spent the rest of the afternoon creating new flyers on his computer. He could smell the chicken and greens cooking. While he printed the flyers, Jumper thought about his other problem. It was five thirty. Soon, Marcus and Nia would arrive.

Jumper lay across his bed playing video games. When the doorbell rang, Jumper rolled off his bed, raced down the steps, and looked through the peephole in the door. Then he yanked it open.

"Hey," he said, trying to sound casual.

"Hey," Marcus replied as Jumper stepped back to let him in.

"Where's Nia?"

"Couldn't make it," Marcus said.

"Oh," Jumper murmured awkwardly. *Now what?* he thought. "Uh, do you want to play some video games?"

"Sure," Marcus replied.

"Guess I should check with my grandmother first. She may have dinner ready," Jumper said. He signaled for Marcus to follow him into the kitchen.

"Well, don't you look nice!" Miss BB said as soon as the boys walked into the kitchen.

"Thank you," Marcus replied.

Jumper checked his clothes. Marcus was dressed in khaki pants and a blue-and-white button-down shirt. His shoes were polished.

"Where's your sister?" Miss BB asked Marcus.

He shuffled his feet. "She wanted to come," he began. "My dad . . . well, my dad wouldn't let her."

"That's too bad," Miss BB said. She sensed that there was more to the story, but didn't want Marcus to feel uncomfortable.

Marcus looked up. He nodded.

"Grandma, how long before dinner?" asked Jumper.

"Twenty minutes or so. You boys can play until then. I'll call you," she replied.

"Come on," Jumper said. He led the way to the second floor.

Marcus stood at the top of the steps and looked around. The front room had a desk, a bookcase, a television, a couple of big, comfortable-looking chairs, and a video game setup. There was a bathroom in the middle of the floor and another area with twin beds. "Where does your mother sleep?" he asked.

"Oh, her rooms are upstairs. Want to see?"

Marcus shook his head no. "You mean this whole floor is yours?"

Jumper nodded. He looked around, seeing his space through Marcus's eyes. It *was* a lot. More room than he'd had in his Connecticut house.

"And where does your grandmother sleep?"

"She has an apartment downstairs," Jumper replied, then flopped into one of the chairs and picked up the game controls. "What game do you want to play first?" he asked Marcus.

Marcus wandered over and sank into the second chair.

Jumper handed him several games, which Marcus studied intently. Finally, he handed one back to Jumper. They played for several rounds without saying a word. Marcus finally broke the silence.

"I always wanted to come into one of these houses," he began. "My family and friends all live in apartments. I like this better."

Jumper waited.

"My dad used to talk about getting us a house, but then he got in a car accident and couldn't walk anymore," Marcus said.

"At least he's alive," Jumper said.

Marcus looked over at Jumper. "I hadn't thought about it that way. What's it like not having a father?"

"I miss him," Jumper replied. "I remember having him around and I miss his company. I wake up some mornings thinking I'll ask my dad to take me to play some ball and then remember he's not here. Some nights I can't sleep for missing him so bad," Jumper admitted.

"I guess my dad misses walking, too. Somebody has to carry him and put him into his bed. My mom has to give him a bath. He drinks too much and is mad all the time," Marcus said.

"I can't imagine that," said Jumper. "That must be rough." His dad used to work hard and sometimes he got mad, but mostly he was nice. Really nice.

Marcus stood, shoved his hands in his pockets, and walked slowly to the windows. Jumper's neighbors sat on their stoop playing cards. Another family jumped rope in front of their house. He could see through the windows into the house across the street. Children and adults were in the living room together.

"Nia and my dad had an argument tonight. That's why she's not here," he said softly.

"Why'd they argue?"

"It was about me. My father wants me to go to a boarding school. It's a military school for boys who get into trouble," Marcus admitted.

"Did you?" Jumper asked.

"What?"

"Did you get into trouble?"

"I got kicked out of school, didn't I?" Marcus replied. He sounded annoyed.

Jumper paused, then decided to go for it. "Why'd you get kicked out?" he asked.

"Some kids stole the seventh-grade entrance test," Marcus told him. "One kid said I did it. The nuns kicked me out."

"Did you do it?"

Marcus turned and faced Jumper. "No."

"Did you tell the nuns that?"

"Of course, but who listens to me?" Marcus turned back to the window.

"Nia," Jumper replied, thinking of how she'd come to her brother's defense.

"True. That's why she got in trouble tonight," said Marcus.

Jumper got up and joined him at the window. "Is she okay?"

"She's mad, that's all."

"Bet you are, too," Jumper said.

"I was so mad! If Mom hadn't pushed me out of the apartment, I wouldn't be here, either!" Marcus snarled.

"I bet," Jumper said. "What are you going to do?"

"Not sure. Go away to school, I guess."

"Jumper," Carolyn called down from the third floor.

"Yes, Mom," Jumper called back.

"Did your friends get here?"

"Marcus is here," he called up to his mom. "Nia's not coming."

"Oh, that's too bad. Anyway, I'll be right down. Go check with your grandmother and see if she needs any help," his mom said.

Jumper looked back at Marcus. "My mom's an artist. She uses the front of her floor as a studio. She must be working on something now. Come on. We better go help my grandmother."

They raced down the steps. Jumper landed seconds before Marcus.

"Food's almost ready. Set the table," Miss BB instructed.

Jumper gave Marcus the plates. He took the silverware. While they worked, Jumper and Marcus rehashed their recent loss to the girls.

"Man, your sister can move!" Jumper admitted.

Marcus laughed. "She's been running from me for years."

"I didn't know she could shoot like that."

"She checked out your jump shot and came home begging me to help her. Guess I taught her too well," he said.

"Just don't help her with her speech," Jumper replied.

"Don't worry. Nia won't ask my advice on speaking, but you can bet she'll be ready. Are you?" Marcus asked.

"Getting there."

"Think you can beat Nia?"

"I hope so," Jumper said.

"Me, too."

"You want me to beat your sister?" Jumper asked, surprised.

"I'm tired of Nia winning everything," Marcus replied, still sore about the basketball game. "Won't hurt her to lose the election."

"Will you help me campaign?" asked Jumper.

"Sure. Just don't tell Nia."

Table set, the boys returned to the kitchen.

"Marcus, do you like good old-fashioned Southern cooking?" Miss BB asked.

"If that means fried chicken, I do," he replied.

"And cornbread, macaroni and cheese, and greens!"

"Plus, she baked an apple pie!" Jumper threw in.

"Smells good!" Jumper's mother said as she entered the kitchen. "Marcus, you look so handsome!"

"Thank you, Mrs. Breeze."

"Where's Nia?" she asked.

"She had to stay home," Marcus replied.

"Tell her what happened," Jumper urged. "My mom can figure anything out."

"Not until we're all seated at the table and have said grace," Miss BB insisted. "My dinner's getting cold!"

Once everyone was settled, Miss BB gave thanks and they dug into the food.

"Delicious, Mother," Mrs. Breeze said.

"Sure is," Marcus agreed.

"You're the best, Grandma."

"All right, enough with the compliments. Marcus, you were about to tell us about Nia. Did something happen to her?" Miss BB asked.

"She and my dad had an argument and he wouldn't let her go anywhere," Marcus reported.

"That's too bad. I'm sure she's disappointed," Mrs. Breeze said. "I've never met your parents," she added.

"No. They don't go out much. My dad's in a wheelchair and hates to go out of the house," Marcus said.

"That must be hard on everyone. He can't be happy staying at home all the time," Miss BB said.

"It is hard. Mom goes to work and church. That's about all."

"Marcus's dad wants him to go to a military school," Jumper told them.

"Oh? How do you feel about that?" Miss BB asked.

"Some days I'd like to go just to get out of the house. But I don't want to go away to school," he said.

"What church does your mom go to?" asked Miss BB.

"The Baptist one on 145th Street and Convent," Marcus replied.

"I go there, too. I'll look for her next Sunday," Miss BB suggested. "It's time to stop all this talking and finish eating. Then Jumper and I challenge you and Mrs. Breeze to a Scrabble match. You ready?" Miss BB asked Marcus.

The boys looked at each other and slapped high five.

"Bring it on!" Jumper yelled.

CHAPTER ELEVEN

Monday morning was worse than Jumper had imagined. When he arrived at school, Jumper saw a group of kids standing on the steps. They stopped talking as he approached.

"Loser!" Jacob greeted him.

"Pretty sad," another boy chimed in, shaking his head.

"I think I'll vote for Nia. Talk about drive! She's got it. She wants it! She's gonna win it!" a girl added.

"Nia got lucky," Jumper shot back.

"Well, maybe she'll get lucky again on election day," another girl said.

Jumper smiled. "We'll see," he said, and slid through the school door. He was so happy to see Mr. Wright.

"Took some ribbing, huh?" he greeted Jumper.

"You heard?"

"I caught some of it," he admitted. "See you at practice."

Jumper spotted Nia heading toward him and ducked into an empty classroom.

"What's the matter, Jumper?" Nia asked as she peeked inside the classroom.

Jumper was looking at the bulletin board like he meant to be there. "Oh, hi, Nia. Sorry you missed dinner on Saturday."

"Yeah, right. You don't have to hide, Jumper. It's over, anyway. I've got this election sewed up!" She laughed and waltzed out of the classroom.

Jumper waited a minute, then followed her out. He made it to his locker without too much trouble.

"Hey," Kelvin greeted him. He was leaning up against Jumper's locker. "It ain't pretty," he said.

"No, it's not. I just saw Nia. She thinks the elections are a done deal," Jumper said.

"She would, but Coach Wright gave me a great idea," Kelvin said. He handed Jumper a DVD.

"What's this?"

"It's the game."

"So? What's that got to do with the elections?" Jumper asked.

"Thought you could use it with your speech," Kelvin replied.

"Huh?"

"I'll tell you about it later," Kelvin said. "And don't worry about the game. By Saturday, no one's mind will be on it. You'll be blowing them away with your dancing feet!"

"Saturday," Jumper groaned. "I hope this whole dance tournament doesn't turn out to be another mistake."

"Don't worry. It's all about having fun and making new friends. Wait 'til we bust through the curtain in our costumes!" Kelvin added.

Costumes were part of the fun. Jumper and Kelvin had gone on the Web and studied the video dance characters. The whole character thing was part of the video dance craze culture. Fans had favorites and were very critical of costumes.

When the boys had picked out their characters, Jumper's mom took them shopping in secondhand clothing shops and costume stores until their outfits were together.

"Mom thinks we should practice in them. Can you come over this afternoon?" Jumper asked.

"Sure."

"Good. Marcus is coming, too. He's been to a lot of dance tournaments and wants to show us some moves," Jumper said.

"Bet. See ya after school," Kelvin replied.

Jumper, Marcus, and Kelvin met up later that afternoon at the Breezes' brownstone. Jumper and Kelvin went upstairs to change into costume. When they were ready, they strutted down to show Marcus and Jumper's mother.

"You look amazing!" Mrs. Breeze shouted and clapped.

"Very cool," Marcus said in agreement.

"Are you sure? I can't afford to embarrass myself," Jumper said. He felt ridiculous.

"Me, neither," Kelvin chimed in, nervous over his costume and routine.

"I'm sure you'll be great," Jumper's mom told the boys. "I'll leave you to practice and wait until Saturday to see the performance."

"Thanks, Mom," said Jumper.

"Yes, thank you, Mrs. Breeze. The costumes are hot!" Kelvin chimed in.

After she'd left, Marcus took over. "Okay, show me what you've got." Jumper got out his video game and dance pad that was designed to be used at home. It wasn't as fancy or high-tech as the ones in the arcades, but it worked. When you hit the arrows, they lit up. Marcus started up the song Jumper had selected for his routine.

Jumper stepped up to the dance pad and began his routine. For the next minute and a half, he stepped to the beat, mixing double steps and jumps with spins and just a few missteps.

When the song ended, Jumper flopped to the floor, out of breath.

Marcus pounced. "You need to pick it up. You're looking at the screen too much. It's throwing off your step. Try it again. And this time, add a flip," he told Jumper.

"A flip! Are you crazy?"

"Well, you can jump, can't you?" Marcus asked.

Jumper repeated his routine until he could do it without relying too much on the screen in front of him. With that change, his movements were quick and fluid. He jumped into the air and landed square on the arrow.

"You're ready," Marcus said.

Jumper wiped the sweat pouring off his face with a towel; his T-shirt was soaked. "Thanks," he said.

"Your turn," Marcus said to Kelvin.

Kelvin stood, stretched, then took his position with his legs spread across two blocks. "Ready," he said, as the room rocked from the deep bass sounds.

Jumper and Marcus watched Kelvin's smooth dance movements. His feet were quick, his hands fluid. He danced to a faster beat, which kept his feet moving so fast that the routine looked more difficult than it was. Kelvin concluded with a split!

Marcus made some minor adjustments to Kelvin's routine. He practiced a few more times, then they called it quits for the day.

"I wonder who's helping Nia?" Jumper asked when they were going over the last details for Saturday's performance. They had plans that went beyond the dance contest. This was all about the campaign.

"All I know is that she's practicing with her dance teacher," Marcus told him.

"Her dance teacher!" Jumper repeated.

"Yeah, Nia's been taking classes at the YMCA since she was five. She's good, too," Marcus told them.

"What character did she pick?" Kelvin asked.

"Who cares?" Marcus interrupted. "You'll see on Saturday."

"He's right," Jumper said. "Let's just make sure we're ready."

"I think we are!" Kelvin declared.

The days that followed were filled with school, basketball, campaigning, and the dance tournament. On Friday, Jumper and Kelvin handed out new flyers. The graphic was a video dance pad in bright colors with Jumper's slogan boldly printed across the straight line of the arrows. At the bottom, they gave the details of the dance tournament.

Saturday turned out to be a warm, sunny day. It was too nice to be cooped up in an arcade, but that didn't stop the kids from Langston Hughes from flocking in. The arcade was filled!

The computer software company staged the tournament. The dancers, six in all, were all newcomers to the scene.

The kids gathered around the dance pad. It was partitioned off by a rope fence. A curtain was set up to give the effect of a real stage.

Adults were there, too — mostly parents and friends of the dancers. Jumper peeked through the curtain to see the crowd. His mother and grandmother stood in the front alongside Kelvin's mom and dad. He was very nervous.

Juston had signed on to be the emcee. He was responsible for the music and introductions. A man from the software company was the scorekeeper. Each dancer had a warm-up song before the one that counted.

Kelvin was up first.

Kelvin stepped from behind the curtain. He wore white boots, a black T-shirt with yellow stripes, black pants, a black helmet with yellow stripes, and blue goggles on top of the helmet.

"Astro!" the kids shouted, recognizing his character. Kelvin strutted onto the dance pad, then broke into his first routine and immediately into his second. Kelvin stepped forward, back, and side to side in time to the beat. He hit the arrows without missing a step. When he jumped, then landed in a split, Kelvin heard the kids shouting: "Woof! Woof! Woof!"

He bowed to the crowd and walked off into the audience. Three other kids took their turns next.

Nia, dressed as Lady, was the fifth performer. She sashayed onto the dance floor flaunting tight purple pants, a wide white belt, and white tennis shoes.

The music started. Nia cartwheeled across the pad; her hands landed on the top right arrow. It lit up. Her feet touched the back two arrows at the same time in sync to the music. She spun around, making several revolutions to the enthusiastic cheering from the crowd.

The crowd shouted: "Nia! Nia! Nia!"

Nia smiled brightly. Years of ballet had paid off! She bowed and left the dance floor.

Kelvin appeared and ran back and forth in front of the dance floor. He waved a big sign that read: JUMP UP JUMPER, JUMP UP! JUMP UP JUMPER, JUMP UP! Kelvin got the whole crowd chanting.

The chants got louder, stronger. Suddenly the curtains flew apart and Jumper strutted onto the dance pad dressed in a bright green old-style suit with a red tie, red tennis shoes, a purple Afro wig, and a fake black mustache. The crowd roared. "Afro!"

As the music kicked in, Jumper started off slow:

Up, up, right, back
Up, left, back, right
Back, back, right, back...

As the music picked up, so did his steps:

Left, back, right, back, left, left, back
Back, forward, left, right, left, back, forward, right
Left, back, forward, left, left, back, back, right, right...

Sweat poured down Jumper's face. The Afro wig took the temperature up several degrees. He stepped right, left, back, forward so fast that his feet tripped him up and he tumbled to the mat.

Laughter rocked the crowd.

Jumper hopped up and began again.

He tapped the arrows with his toes, spun around, and leapt into the air, lighting the arrows as his feet hit the pad. The crowd clapped and cheered. The kids loved it. They shouted: "Jump up for Jumper!"

He jumped high into the air, thrilling the crowd, spun around, and landed with both feet on the right arrow. Jumper ended his performance with a backflip, hitting the right and left arrows with his feet!

The crowd quieted when the judge stepped forward with the scores.

"Congratulations to all the dancers," the judge began. "This contest was judged in three areas: costume, dance steps, and crowd response. Our winner is Afro!"

Jumper ran up to claim his prize as the crowd roared: "Jump up for Jumper!"

CHAPTER TWELVE

On Sunday, Jumper, Marcus, Kelvin, and Eddie sat in Jumper's living room debating about his upcoming speech.

"Can you dunk, man?" Marcus asked Jumper.

"What's that got to do with anything?"

"Can you?" Marcus repeated.

"Sure. Can you?" Jumper shot back.

"Test me," Marcus said.

"What, now?"

"Right now. Let's go to the park so you can show me your stuff," Marcus said.

"Marcus, the election is tomorrow! We've got to stay focused," Kelvin cried.

"We are," Marcus replied.

"What's dunking got to do with getting Jumper elected?" Eddie asked, annoyed with the interruption.

"I'll let you figure it out," Marcus said.

They'd been arguing for the past thirty minutes on a theme for Jumper's speech. Kelvin wanted to stick with *Jump up for Jumper.* Marcus thought it was weak. Eddie just wanted a decision. Time was running out. Instead, he got a slam dunk contest. Go figure!

"You didn't dunk in the last game," Marcus continued to push Jumper.

"Neither did you," he fought back.

"If I had, you'd say I was showing off," he replied.

"Got that right," Jumper said.

"Well, then," Marcus said.

"It wasn't that kind of game," Jumper defended.

"And who won?" Marcus threw back.

"You think if I'd thrown a couple of dunks we would have won?"

"I'm not saying that."

"Then what?"

"If you'd fought harder, we'd have won," Marcus said.

"You kept hogging the ball," Jumper reminded him.

"Trying to get you to work harder, that's all," Marcus said, laughing.

"So you helped us blow the game to teach me a lesson?" Kelvin jumped in.

"Too bad it didn't work," Marcus said.

"Marcus, you're too strange for me," Jumper said in disgust. "This is a waste of time!"

"Trust me," Marcus said.

"Why should I?" Jumper asked, suddenly regretting involving Marcus in his campaign push.

"You want to win, right?"

"What do you know about winning a campaign?" Eddie asked.

"I've been fighting all my life. The fact that I'm still here is a win. Same with Nia," he replied. "Let's go!" he said, standing.

Jumper shot Kelvin a pleading look as Marcus waited for an answer.

"Let's get it over with," Kelvin finally said.

"All right," Jumper said, accepting the challenge. "Let's go!"

Jumper grabbed his basketball, told his mom where they were going, and headed outside with the others. It was a cool, cloudy day. Folks had hoodies on. Jumper, Kelvin, Eddie, and Marcus wore only T-shirts and jeans. They walked fast, fighting off the chill.

"That court's empty," Kelvin pointed out as they reached the park.

The foursome sauntered over to the court. They shot baskets and warmed up before Kelvin and Eddie stepped back.

"Let the contest begin," Kelvin called out as soon as he and Eddie were a safe distance away.

"You ready?" Marcus asked Jumper.

"Ready!" Jumper replied.

"Five chances. One with the most dunks wins," Marcus called out.

Jumper was suddenly nervous. He hadn't even attempted a dunk since his father died. What if he couldn't do it anymore?

He dribbled around the court before racing toward the basket, leaping into the air, and attempting a dunk. One down. Three more failed attempts followed. The ball made it through the hoop, but his hand never touched the rim.

Disgusted, Jumper fought his urge to quit.

He avoided looking at Marcus.

Then Jumper lifted high into the air, threw the ball down, and dangled from the rim with his right hand! He fell to the ground.

Marcus slapped Jumper high five. He took the ball from Jumper and warmed up his arms and legs by dribbling around the court. At five-nine, Marcus had Jumper by two inches. He took a few practice shots before announcing, "The next one counts!"

Jumper stood back watching. Marcus was taller, older, and obviously more experienced. Still, it took three tries before he dunked the ball and hung from the rim with two hands.

As he landed, Kelvin, Eddie, and Jumper circled him.

"Nice job," Kelvin told them. "But I still don't get the point. What did you prove?"

Jumper looked at Kelvin, smiling. "That I could," he said. "I'm ready to go back to my house and start working. I plan to win!"

Kelvin whooped.

They stopped for sodas and chips at the corner store, then flopped on couches in the living room.

Jumper's mom came out of the kitchen with snacks. "That was a quick trip to the park," she said. "Were the courts full?"

"No. Marcus wanted to prove a point," Jumper said.

Mrs. Breeze looked at Marcus. "What was that?"

"Jumper said he could dunk. I needed to see it," Marcus said.

"Did you?"

"He did the best one-handed dunk," Eddie told her.

"That's good. But did you go all the way to the park just to see him dunk the ball?"

Marcus nodded. "Yes," he replied.

Mrs. Breeze looked at her son. "Now that I think about it, I haven't seen you dunk the ball since your father died," Mrs. Breeze said. "You know, people use the term 'slam dunk' off the court, too," she continued.

"Like what, Mom?" Jumper asked.

"They use it to describe their success or say 'it's a slam dunk' when they think they have a good chance of success," she replied.

Jumper glanced at Marcus. "This is all starting to make sense," he said.

"Yeah, like Nia's attitude. She's acting like it's a slam dunk that she'll win the elections," Kelvin said.

"We can't let her," Jumper said. "I can't let her. Mom, could we use your easel?"

"Of course."

Jumper and Kelvin ran up the steps to the third floor and retrieved the easel, a big pad of paper, and some colored markers. They came back down and Jumper took over.

"Okay, we need a new flyer. I came up with one over the weekend, but it won't work. I want something new. Got any ideas?" he asked the group.

"It's got to have color," Kelvin suggested.

"Yeah, and graphics," Marcus said.

"A new slogan," Kelvin reminded them.

"I agree," Jumper said. "Let's start with the graphic. Got any ideas, Marcus?"

"Something basketball," he replied. "Like Michael Jordan dunking the ball, except we put Jumper's face in place of Michael's face."

"Great idea!" Kelvin called out.

"We could do a new poster with the same message. Maybe use a series of photos leading up to the dunk," Eddie suggested.

"I got it!" Marcus shouted. "A vote for Jumper is a SLAM DUNK!"

"That's it!" Jumper said, slapping Marcus a high five.

"Yeah. You can use that in your speech, too," Kelvin added.

While the kids talked, Mrs. Breeze sketched the concept using blue, red, and brown markers.

"That's it!" Kelvin said as the poster mock-up came to life.

"It's all good," Jumper said. "Is that enough?"

"I think you need more," Eddie suggested. "I once heard of this girl who, on election day, made small signs with her name on them and posted them everywhere, including on the bathroom stalls. What about that?"

Jumper worked out the details and they divided up the work. Jumper worked with his mom and Eddie on the third floor designing the poster and name signs while Marcus and Kelvin got on the Internet searching for photos of Michael Jordan in the midst of a dunk.

Two hours later, they were eating pizza and replacing Michael Jordan's face with Jumper's photo.

"Brilliant!" Mrs. Breeze exclaimed as the first prints came out of the printer. She passed the paper around to get everyone's approval.

"It's fun! Should get lots of laughs when everybody at school sees what we've done," Kelvin said.

"Works for me," Jumper told his mom.

"Can't wait to see it blown up," Kelvin agreed with the others.

Marcus studied the doctored photo. "Should his face be larger than the body?" he wondered aloud.

"What's that, Marcus?"

Marcus looked up at Jumper's mom. "I was wondering if Jumper's face should be bigger."

"You mean out of proportion to the body?" Mrs. Breeze asked.

"Hey, he's got a good idea," Kelvin agreed.

Jumper shrugged. "Why?"

"So you'll stand out," Marcus replied.

"Oh, course!" Eddie chimed in. "Michael Jordan's body, big basketball move, Jumper's face!"

"He always did have a big head!" Kelvin said, giving a thumbs-up for the idea.

Mrs. Breeze was already at the computer adjusting the image. She printed it out and handed it to her son.

"If I didn't have a big head before, I've got one now!"

While Jumper and his crew were brainstorming, Nia was chilling.

"Your original slogan was lame," Dakota told Nia. "We need something stronger."

"Does it matter?" Nia asked, sounding bored with the whole process.

"Of course it matters. You've got to stay in the game right to the finish," Dakota reminded her.

"I'm gonna win, Dakota," Nia announced. "Everyone's talking about it."

"Don't be too sure. Jumper has a way of coming back strong. Look what he did at the dance tournament."

"Yeah, he can do a backflip. Big deal. So can I."

"It wasn't just the backflip. It's something else about him that gets people excited."

"Whose side are you on, Dakota?"

"Look, Nia, I just want you to win. That's all."

"I got my speech ready."

"Let's at least make up some new flyers or something," Dakota insisted.

"No. I'm all good," Nia replied stubbornly.

"Do you want to go over your speech?"

"No, thanks," Nia said.

"All right. Well, I've got to get home and babysit my sister," Dakota said.

"Wish me luck," Nia called after her friend.

Dakota looked back, barely smiling. "Luck!" she said.

Nia arrived the next morning dressed in a turquoise blouse and khaki slacks. She stood on the steps and greeted sixth graders as they came into the building.

"Don't forget to vote for Nia," she reminded them with a cheery smile.

"We got ya covered," Callie told her.

That was all the reassurance Nia needed. After chatting with a few more kids, she left her post and walked into school. Nia worked the hallway as she made her way to the auditorium. Jumper's posters and flyers lined the walls, but there was no sign of him.

She stopped to talk to Dakota and Sabrina.

"Have you seen Jumper?" Nia asked.

"Not yet, but I've seen his new poster . . . *everywhere*," Dakota replied. "Kids are loving the whole Jordan body, Jumper face thing."

"You worry too much, Dakota," Nia scolded.

"Don't worry, be happy, right, Nia?" Sabrina asked.

"Today's election day. Let it happen."

"You got it. Now give a good speech!" Dakota told her.

Nia strolled into the auditorium. It was already

crowded with kids. She high-fived and laughed all the way down the aisle. Principal Young called her onto the stage.

"You're up first," she said. "Dakota told us that you didn't have any AV needs, right?"

"That's right, Mrs. Young," Nia replied.

"How long is your speech?"

"About three minutes," Nia told her.

"All right. Have a seat up here. We're starting in five minutes."

Nia sat down on one of the chairs and looked down at her classmates. She smiled and folded her hands in her lap on top of her speech.

Principal Young made a couple of announcements about how the elections would run. "There is a ballot on each of your seats. After the candidates speak, mark your choice and place your ballot in the boxes Miss King and Mr. Wright are holding as you exit the auditorium," she instructed the students. "I'll announce the winners over the loudspeaker before the end of the day. Remember, class, this is not a popularity contest. Vote for the student you think will do the most for your school!

"Our sixth-grade candidates for student council are Nia Johnson and Elijah Breeze, Jumper to you. Nia will speak first." Principal Young stepped back as the girl approached the podium.

Nia placed her papers on the podium and took hold of the mic.

"Good morning, girls and boys. I'm Nia Johnson. I know most of you. For those that don't know me well, I'm here to assure you I'll get your voice heard. I may be short, but I have a loud voice. I want to represent . . ."

Nia droned on for several minutes. She spoke in a monotone and talked about her accomplishments and her ideas in flat sentences. She took the students' silence as a positive sign.

"And so I hope that I've erased any doubts in your mind about my ability to make a difference for Langston Hughes. A vote for Nia is a vote for you! Thank you for your attention and support." Nia nodded.

Dakota clapped loudly and a bunch of students joined in. A few whistled and cheered as Nia took her seat.

Then the lights went down. Music blared from speakers on the stage. A film screen lowered. Suddenly, scenes from the boy/girl basketball game rolled in fast motion across the screen — Jumper's free throws straight through Nia's last basket.

As the ball lifted into the air, the video stopped, and Jumper made his entrance.

Jumper dribbled a basketball across the stage. He was dressed in a girl's pink basketball uniform and wore high-heeled sneakers and a pony-tailed wig! The students roared!

Jumper stopped dribbling as if he were surprised by their presence. He turned to the students with a look of mock horror and shouted, "Oops!"

The students clapped and yelled their approval. Jumper stripped off his uniform, tore off his wig, tossed the ball to Kelvin in the front row, and stepped over to the podium.

"While I couldn't stop Nia's ball from sinking into the net, I can promise you that with Jumper on student council, life here will be *a slam dunk*!"

Then he gave his speech.

Students were still laughing as they filed out of the auditorium and cast their votes. Jumper and Kelvin headed back to class to wait.

"I bet you'll win," Kelvin told Jumper. "It all worked."

"Marcus and my mom worked magic with that video," he replied, "and your idea of the girl's uniform was really funny. You're the best manager!"

"Thanks, man," Kelvin replied.

Jumper met up with Nia on his way to class.

"You were good," she said, slapping him high five. "That whole slam dunk thing was kicking," Nia added.

"Yeah, well, ask your brother about it someday," Jumper told her.

"My brother?"

"It was his idea," Jumper told her.

"He helped you?"

"Yeah."

"You know, he's been different lately. Ever since he came over to your house," Nia said. "No arguing. He's been helpful at home. And now you say he helped you out, too. I don't get it. What happened?"

Jumper thought about her question. *Miss BB*, he thought. *That's what happened.* She'd made a big difference in his life, too. "My grandmother took to Marcus right away. I think she wanted to help him."

"Yeah, Marcus seemed pretty happy about meeting her, too. Hey, you want to have a rematch? Girls against boys?" Nia asked.

"No way," Jumper replied, laughing.

"What, we're too good for you?"

"No. Let's just be friends for a while," he suggested.

"You mean no matter how the vote goes?" Nia asked.

"That's right. Just friends," he repeated.

"Then how 'bout we skip homeroom and go to the office? That way we can hear the news together before the others," Nia suggested.

"Let's go," Jumper said.

"I think you worked harder than me," Nia admitted as they walked toward the principal's office. "Dakota tried to tell me to kick it up a notch, but I didn't listen. I counted too much on my popularity."

"Hey, the vote's not in yet," Jumper reminded her. "And you *are* popular."

Principal Young was coming out of her office as they walked in. "Skipping homeroom, are we?"

Jumper and Nia nodded sheepishly.

"We just had to know who won," said Nia.

The principal laughed. "I'll let you go this one time. Come on in. I've got news."

Jumper and Nia followed her inside.

Jumper stood while Nia sank into the chair across from Mrs. Young. "I'm glad you came in together. It just proves my point. You'd both make good leaders."

"Is the vote in?" Nia asked.

Jumper moved in closer. "Is it?" he joined in.

"We just finished the count," the principal replied.

"Who won?" Jumper asked.

Principal Young leaned back in her chair, smiling.

"Jumper won, didn't he? Just tell us," Nia pleaded.

"I was surprised myself," she began.

"I told you, Jumper," Nia interrupted.

"Not so fast, Nia. Jumper didn't win," she said.

Jumper's head fell. He was disappointed. Nia was right — he'd worked hard and really wanted to win. "Congratulations, Nia," he said, looking back up.

"Thanks, but . . ."

"Hold up. Nia didn't win, either," Principal Young said, chuckling.

"What!"

"That's right, Nia. You and Jumper tied! It looks like the sixth grade will have two representatives!"

Nia leapt out of her chair.

Jumper flew into the air! "I guess you could call that a two-handed slam dunk!"

ABOUT THE AUTHOR

Sharon Robinson is an educational consultant for Major League Baseball. She has written several nonfiction books about her father, baseball legend Jackie Robinson.

Prior to joining Major League Baseball, Ms. Robinson had a 20-year career as a nurse-midwife and educator. She has taught at Yale, Columbia, Howard, and Georgetown universities. She has also served as director of the PUSH for Excellence Program and as a fundraiser for The United Negro College Fund and A Better Chance.